ANNE-MARIE CONWAY is
specialising in drama. She has
theatre company, Full Circle.
her husband, two teenage boys and two eccentric cats,
Betty and Boo.

She is an award-winning author of six acclaimed novels,
including *Butterfly Summer*, which won The Oxfordshire
Book Awards 2013 and has recently been selected as an
Usborne Classic, and *Forbidden Friends*, which won the
Southwark Book Award 2014.

Unicorn Girl is being published to help raise
money to build a new library at a local secondary
school. Anne-Marie is thrilled to be involved in such an
exciting, ambitious and worthwhile project. At a time
when so many libraries are being closed, she cannot
wait to see *Unicorn Girl* – alongside hundreds of other
books – sitting proudly on the shelves of the Archer
Academy library.

'You can find magic wherever you look. Sit back and
relax, all you need is a book!'   – Dr Seuss

Also by Anne-Marie Conway

Butterfly Summer
Forbidden Friends
Tangled Secrets

Unicorn Girl

Anne-Marie Conway

Dear Kitty,

Best wishes,

Anne-Marie

SilverWood

This book is dedicated to The Archer Academy

Published in 2018 by Eponine Press

ISBN 978-1-9164363-0-5 (paperback)
ISBN 978-1-9164363-1-2 (ebook)

British Library Cataloguing in Publication Data
A CIP catalogue record for this book is available from
the British Library

Page design and typesetting by SilverWood Books
www.silverwoodbooks.co.uk

Printed on responsibly sourced paper

Acknowledgements

Unicorn Girl has had an unusual route to publication and there are many people who have helped it on its journey. A huge 'thank you' to my lovely agent, Julia Churchill, for reading and rereading and rereading. Her insight and advice were invaluable. The wonderful team at SilverWood Books, especially Catherine Blom-Smith for her care and attention throughout. My dear friend, Franda, who leapt on board and offered to design the front cover: I couldn't be more thrilled with the results. My talented niece, Shannon, for the illustrations inside the book – it was truly magical to see the story come to life before my eyes. To Sophie Bristow and Justine Csaky, for their advice and support. To all the girls at Channing Junior School who convinced me that the world needed another unicorn story. My sister Paula for simply being the best. And to Danny, my rock.

Before the Beginning...

Long ago, in far off times, unicorns roamed freely across the lands. These kind and noble creatures could be found in dense woodland, only leaving their homes to find and protect those most in need. Each unicorn was unique, with its own features and personality.

Many people believed that if they were lucky enough to see a unicorn, they would be blessed with good fortune. The hungry would find food, the lonely would find friendship, and the poor would be rewarded.

However, over time, these harmless superstitions took on a sinister twist. A single sighting was no longer enough to satisfy some people. They wanted more than luck. They came to believe that the unicorn's horn was magic – that it could cure the sick, even those who were at death's door.

This put unicorns in grave danger. Specialist hunters would track and kill them with a single arrow to the heart. Once caught and killed, the hunter would chop off the unicorn's horn and grind it into a fine powder. This powder would then be sold to the highest bidder.

Eventually, when only a few unicorns were left, a harsh winter swept the world. It was known as The Deep Freeze. The icy conditions and plummeting temperatures drove the surviving unicorns into hibernation. Easily camouflaged in the snow, they were finally safe from hunters.

The Deep Freeze lasted for many, many years. The unicorns slept on, safe under their soft, snowy blanket. By the time temperatures started to rise and the snow began to melt, no one had seen a unicorn for so long it was widely believed that they had become extinct.

Waking up from their endless sleep, the surviving unicorns found themselves in a world full of forests and fields and tall grassy hills. Taking no chances, they used the magic from their horns to weave an invisible barrier that would protect them from the evil hunters and their deadly arrows.

With spools of transparent twine wound tightly around their horns, they set to work spinning and sewing and knitting and lacing – the fibrous thread leaving a faint, spiral pattern on their once-smooth horns. They didn't stop until they had created a membrane that stretched from the forest floor to the tops of the trees, separating the human world from the unicorn world forever.

From *The Lost Unicorn*
Author unknown

Chapter One

Today was Granny Rae's funeral.

Everyone came dressed in black and sniffed into lace hankies and talked in these really hushed voices as if they were at the library (apart from Baby Boo, who screamed the church down). Granny Rae would've *hated* it. She would have rolled her eyes and clicked her tongue the whole way through.

Mum invited all the relatives back to ours for tea and cake and even more sniffing and whispering. She said it was a good opportunity for the whole family to meet Boo all in one go. She's been putting it off for ages, ever since he came home from hospital. Hardly anyone's been round to see him, apart from the weekly visits from the doctor.

The house was crammed. It was impossible to take more than two steps without some random aunty I hadn't seen for ages saying 'Haven't you *grown,* Ariella!' when everyone knows I haven't grown at all and I'm still the smallest in the class even though I'm in Year 6.

Most annoying of all was my big sister, Trish. She'd tied back her messy, streaked-blonde hair into the neatest ponytail and was busy handing round cups of tea and slices of Victoria sponge, pretending to be perfect, when she wasn't even close to Granny Rae.

I lasted for half an hour before escaping upstairs to my room. This was the first funeral I'd ever been to and I hated everything about it too. Granny Rae should be downstairs, drinking tea and eating cake with the rest of the family. She loved Victoria sponge. We should have thrown her a party *before* she died.

My new room overlooks the back garden and fields beyond. The garden's divided into three sections with a big terrace at the top, a lawn area in the middle and a tangle of ancient trees, tall shrubs and blackberry bushes at the bottom. Dad had grand plans for it when we first looked round the house, but it's been left to grow wild.

I stood at the window, watching the clouds scuttle across the autumn sky. I didn't think anyone would notice I'd disappeared, or be bothered, but a few moments later there was a knock on the door. I ignored it at first, hoping they'd go away. I wasn't in the mood to chit-chat to some relative I didn't even know. But they knocked again, harder.

"Excuse me, Ariella, may I to come in?"

It was Uncle Boris, Granny Rae's oldest friend from Russia, the only one of her close friends still alive. "Those stairs are much more steepier than they look," he said, shuffling into my room, coughing and spluttering into a large, crumpled handkerchief.

Uncle Boris lives in Russia but he comes to England every Christmas to stay with Granny Rae. We've always called him 'Uncle' even though he's not related to us. He's actually more like a grandpa than an uncle, with his thick white hair and matching fluffy beard.

"I have here something for you, Ariella," he said, when he'd got his breath back. "Something from your grandmother."

"Really? From Granny Rae?"

He nodded. "Yes. Something very much precious. She gave it to me before she was dying. Three weeks ago, maybe four, I lose track now."

He reached into the faded satchel he was carrying and pulled out a small velvet jewellery box. "She left it for you with special message: it must not to be opened until *after* funeral."

I stared at him. "What, she actually said that?"

Uncle Boris nodded again.

The last time I saw Granny Rae she was lying in a hospital bed hooked up to a million wires and loud, beeping machines. She looked small and frail like this injured bird I found once on the way home from school. She didn't say anything about a gift, or leaving me something, or special messages.

It's strange when someone dies. You know you're never going to see them again, that they've gone forever. But then you start to think about *forever*, and how it's longer than anything you've ever imagined, too big to work out in your head – like the sky, or the ocean, or outer space. It just goes on and on and on.

Boris handed me the box and I eased it open. For a moment it felt as if Granny Rae was in the room with us. I glanced up at Boris. He was watching me closely. I wondered if he could feel it too. Inside the box, sitting on a satin cushion, was a long, silver chain with an antique unicorn charm hanging in the middle.

"Granny Rae's unicorn charm," I breathed. "She showed it to me once when I was at her house." I lifted it out of the box and Boris helped me to clasp it around my neck.

"It look lovely," he said. His eyes were blurry. "It will be bringing you luck. Where I come from, it is a sign of luck." I felt like crying too. Granny Rae knew how much I loved unicorns. She knew all about the unicorn games I used to make up with my best friend, Neve, before we moved away. Our unicorn universe where *anything* could happen.

"But I don't understand. Why didn't she give it to me herself? Why did she wait? Now I can't say thank you or tell her how much I love it."

I went over to my dressing table to look at the necklace in the mirror. It felt warm against my skin. I ran my fingers over the unicorn's miniature, swirling mane. "Sometimes it's like Granny Rae's still here." The words burst out of me. "Not just now. Other times as well. And I'm not imagining it."

I knew Uncle Boris wouldn't laugh at me, not like Trish. He smiled through the mirror, his eyes still damp. "If you are needing her, Ariella," he said, "she will never be far."

I helped Uncle Boris back down the stairs, stopping every few steps for him to catch his breath. Close up, I could hear his lungs gurgling like old water pipes. He asked me how I was coping with the move to Baywood, and starting my new school, and living in the countryside. I liked how he asked. Like he was properly interested.

We stopped halfway down for a longer rest and I told him how changing schools was the hardest thing I'd ever done. That I hated my new teacher and I missed my friends, especially Neve. That most mornings I wanted to hide under my covers and pretend I was in my old bedroom in our old house.

I told him all that, but I didn't tell him everything. I didn't tell him how scared I was. I didn't say, 'I know very old people have to die, but do babies sometimes die too?'

My hand went up to the unicorn charm while I was talking. It still felt warm.

"Anyway, I've got this now. You said yourself it would bring me luck. Maybe it's even magic…"

"Magic?" said Uncle Boris. "Is that what you think, Ariella? A magic charm from your Granny Rae?"

When we got to the bottom of the stairs he leaned in close and said something else. I think it was Russian. The only Russian word I know is *Babushka*, which means Granny. I was about to ask him what it meant when Mum popped up next to me, carrying Boo.

"Give me a hand, would you, Ariella? I left the changing bag in the car and he's done a stinker!"

She placed Boo in my arms, warned me to hold him carefully, and rushed off before I could tell her I was in the middle of talking to Uncle Boris. Boo wriggled to get down. He was sticky, as if he'd been at the Victoria sponge, and very smelly. He really had done a stinker. It's something to do with the medication he's taking. If anything could clear the room it was one of Boo's poos.

I hoisted him back up, willing Mum to hurry. She was *ages*. Long enough for two aunties to tell me how much I'd grown and for Uncle Sid to give a big sniff and say Boo might need his nappy changing, as if it wasn't totally obvious. Boo buried his face in my neck. He wasn't used to strangers. I pulled him closer, kissing the top of his head. The smell didn't bother me.

By the time Mum came back there was no sign of Uncle Boris anywhere and I had absolutely no idea what he'd said. I helped change Boo's nappy, distracting him with his favourite beany bear, swooping beany bear down to blow raspberries on his tummy, over and over. He squealed and squirmed and kicked his legs, but at least he didn't start crying again.

People began to leave at around six, but it was another hour before the house was empty. Trish did her best vanishing act the second Mum mentioned clearing up. She suddenly had homework to do, or a test to revise for, or something else vitally important, and *poof!* she was gone. Dad took Boo upstairs for his bath and Mum and I stood at the sink.

The new dishwasher hasn't been plumbed in yet and there were piles of jammy plates and empty tea cups. Mum said she would wash and I should dry. I wasn't sure whether to tell her about the unicorn necklace or to see if she noticed it first. I was worried she might say

Trish should have it because she's the oldest.

"Do you think we'll see Uncle Boris again before he goes back to Russia?" I said instead. "He whispered something to me in Russian before he left and I can't remember what it was."

Mum shook her head. "It's too late, he's gone." She handed me a plate to dry. "He had a taxi waiting to take him straight to the airport."

"*Gone? Already?*" My tummy tightened. "But do you think we'll see him again?"

Mum leaned against the sink. She looked even more exhausted than usual. "Of course we'll *see* him. What do you mean?"

"It's just that he's not our *real* uncle, is he? We're not actually related. He only came to England every year to see Granny Rae and he might think he's not welcome here anymore now that..."

"Ariella! For goodness' sake! Calm down! I've just said, we'll see him. It might not be *this* Christmas. I doubt he'll come back so soon after the funeral..."

Just then Dad staggered into the kitchen as if he'd survived a great battle. He was just as worn out as Mum. "Boo's bathed and in his cot, but he's so overtired I'm not sure how much milk he'll take."

A look passed between them. They thought I didn't notice, but I did. It was the look that meant Boo *had* to have some milk, no matter what.

"I'll try, if you like," I offered, even though I knew Mum would want to do it herself.

"It's okay," said Mum, peeling off her rubber gloves. "You finish up here with Dad."

Dad plunged his hands straight into the soapy water. He made a silly joke that if washing-up was an Olympic event, he'd definitely win gold. He handed me a plate to dry, his eyes falling on the necklace. "Ooh, that's pretty, Ariella." He peered at it more closely. "What is it? A horse?"

A horse? Was that another joke? How could anyone mistake a unicorn for a horse?

As soon as the washing-up was finished, I left Dad in the kitchen and went upstairs. Trish was coming out of the bathroom. She had her earphones in and she was mouthing the words to a song. "What's that?" she said, eyeing the necklace as she passed me. She pulled one earphone out, waiting.

My hand went back up to the charm. "It's from Granny Rae. She gave it to Uncle Boris to give to me."

She made the face she always makes when she doesn't believe me. "Are you sure you didn't just find it in her room?"

Granny Rae came to stay with us a few weeks before she died. Dad cleared the dining room downstairs and put in a bed and chest of drawers. I helped him make it look as much like a proper bedroom as possible, with a new bedspread and pretty pouches of lavender to help her sleep. I haven't set foot in there since she died.

"Why would you even say that?" My hands curled into fists. "Do you really think I'd *steal* something out of Granny Rae's room and then lie about it? You're the only one who would do something horrible like that!"

"*Girls!*" Mum stuck her head round her bedroom door, where Boo sleeps. "*Please!* I've just got him off! Keep it down!"

Trish pushed her earphone back in and flounced off, not exactly slamming her door but not shutting it very quietly either.

"For Christ's sake," muttered Mum. "Could she be any more selfish?"

Mum ducked back into her room without waiting for an answer. It was cold on the landing. I pictured her watching over Boo while he slept. Watching his little chest rise and fall, rise and fall, rise and fall.

Chapter Two

Boo was born exactly eight months ago, on the 25th February, at 6.23 am, weighing 2.72 kg. I know all the details because it was me who ended up filling in the special baby book, *Baby's First Year,* that Mum and I bought together before he was born. I remember the day we chose it, in this little gift shop near the hospital. Mum had just had her second scan and found out she was having a boy.

I couldn't wait to meet my new baby brother and start being a big sister. I made a countdown chart to stick on my bedroom wall and crossed the days off as they passed. Mum's tummy grew and grew. First she felt a flutter like butterfly wings. This was followed by a proper kick. Then, when her tummy was huge, an actual elbow or a foot would shoot out, as if the baby was trying to escape. And finally it was time.

It was an easy birth, everyone said afterwards. No complications. Not even the tiniest hint that something was wrong.

It was the first day back after half-term. The girls in my class rushed around, swapping holiday news, shrieking every time someone walked through the gates. I stood by myself, fiddling with the buttons on my cardigan, wishing I had someone to talk to so it wouldn't look so obvious I was on my own.

Mum and Dad planned the move to Baywood as soon as Mum found out she was pregnant. Our old house wasn't big enough for five, and we couldn't afford somewhere bigger in the same area. They were excited about the extra rooms and bigger garden. Trish didn't mind either. She was nearly sixteen and changing schools for sixth form anyway.

The idea was to move at the beginning of the summer holidays, in July. We were even going to get a dog. Mum promised. She said the garden was perfect. But then Boo was born, and Mum and Dad spent the entire summer at the hospital, and we ended up moving the weekend before school started. I barely had time to say goodbye to Neve before I was sitting in my new classroom at Baywood Primary.

The bell rang and everyone raced for the line, talking and laughing as they streamed by. Belinda Burns pushed past me, bashed me on the head with her bag, and then pretended it had all been a terrible accident. "Oh sorry, *Ariella,* I didn't see you there," she said. "I forgot to look *down*."

I tried to think of something clever to say back, but it was too late. She was already at the front with Faye Parks, pointing at me and cracking up. Faye joined in, cracking up as well, as if it was the funniest thing she'd ever heard. I trailed in behind them, forcing a fake smile on my face, pretending I didn't care.

It was Maths first lesson. Mr Major stood by the whiteboard attempting to explain a new way of doing long multiplication called the Grid Method. It was confusing. You had to multiply all the numbers separately and then put them back together again at the end to get the answer.

He whizzed through the theory and then wrote up some examples for us to copy into our books. I glanced across at Belinda. She had her head down, busy copying the sums. She's the main reason I hate Baywood Primary. She's been on my case since the day I joined, teasing me about being small as if I'm a freak. And it doesn't help that she's the tallest in the class.

While Mr Major droned on about breaking the numbers up into hundreds, tens and units, I thought about Granny Rae and the funeral and my unicorn charm. I doodled 'unicorn' in bubble writing across the blank page in front of me and began to sketch a picture of a unicorn underneath, completely forgetting I was supposed to be copying the sums from the board.

I gave the unicorn a flowing mane and spiral horn, and the softest, kindest eyes. My pencil flew across the page. I added even more detail, shading his glossy mane and swishy tail, slowly bringing him to life. Dainty hooves, a velvet nose, thick lashes to frame his eyes.

When I'd finished drawing I named him The White Warrior. He lived deep in the woods, but ventured out at night when everyone was sleeping. He would wait for me at the bottom of the garden and we'd ride off in the moonlight, away from Bayfield, away from Belinda Burns, away from Mr Major and his stupid, complicated, grid method multiplication—

"*Ariella Gold!* What on earth is this?"

I shrunk back in my chair. I hadn't noticed Mr Major coming over. He stabbed the picture with his finger, about to have one of his major meltdowns.

"You're going to be in Year 7 next year. *Sec-on-da-ry School!* You simply can't afford to waste your time day-dreaming!"

Mr Major is short and round with tufty red hair,

but, deep down inside, he thinks he's a *real* major in the army, barking out orders, ready to attack at any moment. He tore the picture out of my book and stood over my desk waiting for me to start. I quickly copied the sums off the board, even though I had no idea what I was supposed to do next.

By the time the bell rang for break I still hadn't done a single sum. Miss Nightingale said she would stay in with me. She's our teaching assistant and the total opposite of Mr Major. She helped me do three examples and then showed me photos of her new kitten, Smudge.

I told her about Granny Rae's funeral and she gave me a hug and said it was no wonder I couldn't concentrate on long multiplication. "It sounds like you and your granny were really close, Ariella."

I nodded shyly. "My mum always said we were like two peas in a pod and it used to make us laugh because Granny Rae hated peas and so do I."

Miss Nightingale gave me another quick hug and said I should get some fresh air before the bell rang. I wished I could show her my unicorn charm but there's a strict 'no jewellery' policy at Baywood.

There was still five minutes of play left when I got outside. Louise and Anisha were on the netball court practising for their next match and a few of the other girls were doing handstands and round-offs on the field. I was about to ask them if I could watch when Belinda came charging over, dragging Faye behind her.

They stood in front of me with their arms folded across their chests as if they were the Official Playground Police. "How come you've only just come out?" asked Belinda. Her voice was hard as stones.

I stared up at her, blinking through my glasses. She knew exactly why I was late coming out. The whole class knew, thanks to Mr Major.

"Here," she said, as if she was being helpful. "You *dropped* something." She pressed a piece of scrunched-up paper into my hand, grabbed Faye's arm and skipped away, laughing, just as the bell rang for the end of break.

It was the torn-out page from my maths book with the picture of the unicorn. She must've swiped it off Mr Major's desk when he wasn't looking. She'd drawn a speech bubble next to the unicorn's mouth and inside the bubble it said '2 + 2 = 5' with a massive red cross.

My face burned with embarrassment. I ripped the page in half and stuffed it in the first bin I passed on the way to line up. I'd draw another picture in the next lesson. An even better one. I didn't care. I wasn't stupid, whatever Belinda Burns thought. In my old school I was good at maths. Sometimes I even helped Neve if she was stuck.

Just before the end of the day, Mr Major said he had an announcement to make. We would be having a cake sale the following Friday to raise money for some new sports equipment for the Winter Olympics. Everyone had to bring in biscuits or cakes to sell in the playground. "Homemade are always best, of course," he added. "If you've got the time."

I had no idea what the Winter Olympics was, but I knew what I was going to make straight away – Granny Rae's Bakewell tart. We'd made it together loads of times and it was delicious: shortcrust pastry filled with warm raspberry jam and topped with feathery white icing.

Lining up to go home, I heard Anisha and Louise say they were planning to bake their cupcakes at Louise's house the day before the sale. I wanted to ask them if I could join in – of all the girls in the class they seemed the nicest, but even if they said 'yes' I might just be tagging along.

"You'd better make sure your cake isn't *mouldy*, Ariella," whispered Belinda suddenly, pushing into the line right behind me. "You wouldn't want to *poison* anyone." She said the word poison as if *I* was poison and anything I touched would become poison.

"I hope you're not talking, Belinda," said Mr Major sharply. "You know the rules."

"Oh no, sorry Mr Major," said Belinda. "I was just telling Ariella about the *homemade* strawberry cheesecake with *fresh* strawberries that I'm going to bring in next Friday."

"Mmm, cheesecake," said Mr Major, patting his tubby tummy. "My favourite."

Chapter Three

The Apgar test is performed on all babies within a minute of them being born. It's called Apgar because it tests the baby's Appearance (healthy skin colour) Pulse (heartbeat) Grimace response (their reflexes), Activity (muscle tone) and Respiration (breathing rate and effort).

When the doctor listened to Boo's heart, she thought she could detect a murmur. She listened again five minutes later, and then took him away for X-rays and scans and some other tests. Eventually, when all the results came through, she told Mum and Dad that Boo had been born with a hole in his heart.

I stroked his cheek the first time I saw him and he gripped my finger with his tiny hand. I didn't understand. He looked so perfect. How could his little heart have a hole in it? It was difficult to imagine. Was it like a doughnut? Or a bagel? Or one of those frisbees with the middle missing?

The proper medical name for the hole was 'ventricular septal defect'. The doctor explained that it was more like a tear than an actual hole and that the one in Boo's heart was on the large side. She said there was a small possibility the tear might repair itself over the next few months, but if that didn't happen he would need a special operation to sew it up.

Dad was up a ladder in the kitchen when I got home. "Don't touch anything, Ariella," he said, waving a paintbrush at me. "Wet paint!" I looked around. The kitchen was half white, half lemony-yellow. The yellow was the old colour. By the time Dad finished the room it would all be gone.

I squeezed round the ladder to where the recipe books were still packed away in a box, glancing at Boo's feeding chart on the fridge door as I passed. It hadn't changed for days, not even by a single gram.

"Do you think Mum's got Granny Rae's recipe for Bakewell tart written down somewhere? You know, the one she used to make with raspberry jam. We've got a cake sale at school next Friday."

Dad stared at me for a moment, as if he was thinking about Granny Rae, or maybe about the recipe and where it might be, but then I realised he wasn't staring *at* me at all – he was staring right through me. "Pass me that pot of paint, would you, love? It's on the table behind you. I've missed a spot just here."

I handed Dad the paint and went upstairs to find Mum. She might know where the recipe was, or maybe even remember it off-by-heart. She was in her room slumped against the wall while Boo shuffled around on his bottom, whimpering, his face streaked with tears.

"Oh look, it's your favourite sister!" she said. Boo stopped and turned towards the door. His face broke into a watery smile. "Take over for a bit, would you, Ariella, love? He's been like this for the past hour and I could really do with a break."

"Mum, I just need to ask you something."

"Later, Ariella, I promise. I'm desperate for a cup of tea, and look, he's so pleased to see you. Read him a story or something. He needs to calm down before his next feed."

She gave my shoulder a grateful squeeze as she left the room. I wanted to tell her about getting into trouble in Maths and Mr Major tearing my picture out of my book and the bake sale next Friday and Belinda saying I was going to poison everyone. I wondered if she missed our after-school chats as much as I did.

I sat on the floor, pulling Boo onto my lap. He was still wearing a Babygro, more like a newborn than an eight-month-old. I reached for his favourite picture book, *Ricky the Rocking Horse*, and he relaxed into me, clutching his beany bear in one hand and turning the pages with the other.

Ricky the Rocking Horse is about a rocking horse who goes on imaginary journeys. He visits the seaside and a fairground, and even travels into space, although, in reality, he never goes anywhere at all. Just rocks backwards and forwards, backwards and forwards in the children's nursery, day after day after day.

Boo's favourite bit is when Ricky goes to the seaside. He paddles in the sea and talks to a crab and eats an ice cream. At one point the crab jumps on his back and says, *'Giddy up, Ricky! Giddy up!'* Boo always tries to say it himself, even though it comes out sounding more like 'Gi-u! Gi-u!'

Halfway through the story I heard Trish come home, open the fridge, close it and then start arguing with Dad about her phone. It was the same argument they had most days. Trish couldn't go more than two minutes without using her phone and Dad couldn't stand it. Their voices got louder and louder until Boo pressed his hands over his ears and began to cry.

I cuddled him close, whispering "*Giddy up, Ricky! Giddy up!*" to distract him, but he banged his head against my chest, working himself up into a state. Mum must've had the monitor on. She'd only been downstairs for five minutes but she came racing back up, scooping Boo out of my lap. "It's okay," she said gently, kissing his tears away. "It's okay, Mummy's here." She walked round the room, patting his back and rocking him until he calmed down.

"Shall I finish the story now?" I reached my arms up for him. "He was really enjoying it."

Mum shook her head, mouthing at me that I could go. I stood outside on the landing listening to her talk to Boo, her voice soft and low. Trish was properly shouting at Dad now, yelling at him to butt out of her life. Mum would go mad if Boo started crying again, not that Trish would care. I ducked into my room and closed the door.

I'd hidden my unicorn necklace at the back of my bedside drawer just in case Trish tried to steal it. I took it out and fastened it around my neck. It was even more beautiful than I remembered. I touched the charm, wishing that Granny Rae was still alive, and that we still lived in our old house, and that Boo would magically get better so that everything could go back to the way it was before.

I heard Trish come storming upstairs swearing at Dad. Dad came storming up after her. Boo began to cry again and Mum flung her door open and screamed at them both to shut up. I put my hands over my ears, like Boo, to block out the noise. It was horrible. I'd never heard Trish actually *swear* at Dad, or Mum say shut up like that.

A weird tingling feeling began to run up and down my arms, like the worst case of pins and needles. I tried to take a breath but there wasn't enough air. My heart was beating too fast. The tingling grew stronger. A loud humming filled my ears and the room tilted. Granny Rae was gone forever. Boo was going to die. Nothing would ever be the same again.

Tears flooded my eyes. It was harder and harder to take a breath. There was no oxygen. I was suffocating. I stumbled over to the window fumbling with the lock, frantic to open it, frantic to let some air in, but it wouldn't budge. It was stuck. I grasped the handle and shook it and rattled it, slamming my hand against the frame, thumping it as hard as I could, over and over, desperate for air.

Then something caught my eye.

A sudden movement through the trees at the bottom of the garden.

A flash of white in the field beyond.

And everything stopped.

Chapter Four

I pressed my palms up against the window, my breath misting up the glass. I used my sleeve to wipe it, blinking my tears away. The noise on the landing was muted now, as if someone had turned the volume down. I was in a dream but wide awake. There was a unicorn in the field. A dazzling-white, *real live* unicorn, just like the one in my picture.

The trees swayed in the wind. The winter sun was low in the sky. I squinted to see more clearly. I stared so hard my eyes began to blur. I was scared if I looked away, even for a moment, he would disappear, vanish into thin air. He was standing very still, looking up at the window, watching me just as closely as I was watching him.

We stayed like that for what felt like a hundred years, our eyes locked together, until eventually the noise from the landing crashed back through, breaking the spell. The unicorn tossed his head, as if he could sense the tension in the house, and took off around the field.

"Don't go," I whispered, resting my head against the windowpane. "Please don't go." I squeezed my eyes closed, too frightened to look. When I opened them again he'd galloped a complete circle and was in the same spot as before, his eyes fixed on mine, as if to say, 'Come on then, what are you waiting for?'

I raced down the garden as fast as I could, tripping and stumbling over molehills and random clumps of weeds, praying the unicorn would still be there, that I hadn't imagined the whole thing. I only looked back once; a darting glance over my shoulder, but there was no sign of Mum or Dad. They hadn't noticed me slip out, and it would be ages before they realised I'd gone.

When I got to the bottom I picked my way through a prickly gap in one of the blackberry bushes, doing my best to dodge the thorny stems and stinging nettles, and then climbed over the wire fence that separates our garden from the field. My cardigan caught on the wire. I felt it pull and tear. I was out of breath and covered in scratches and damp twigs, but it didn't matter. Nothing mattered except seeing the unicorn.

He looked completely different up-close. His dazzling-white coat was actually speckled with grey spots and he was smaller than I'd expected, as if he hadn't finished growing yet. He had knobbly knees, a stumpy horn and his mane was a knotted mess. But his eyes were beautiful – puddles of deep purple ink.

Everything around us had become silent. The only thing I could hear was the soft rush of breath coming from the unicorn's nose. "Hello," I whispered. "I saw you from my bedroom window, up there." He raised his head and looked towards the house, as if he understood, as if we were actually communicating with each other.

I stayed very still, my back pressed against the fence. I didn't want to do anything that might scare him off.

We stood watching each other for a long time. Or maybe it was only a few moments. Time didn't seem to be real anymore. I didn't care about Dad arguing with Trish, or the cake sale, or Belinda Burns. It all felt far away and not massively important.

Eventually I moved towards him, just a few steps. I reached my hand out, but he startled, tossing his head as he took off around the field again. His movements were jerky and uncoordinated, his gangly legs and oversized hooves pulling in different directions, his tail swishing behind him.

He went all the way round twice and then came to a stop close to where I was standing. He was blowing hard through his nose now, his mane sticking up all over the place like it needed a good brush. I stood still as a statue, waiting for him to settle. I wanted to show him he could trust me.

More time passed.

It was cold without my coat.

My legs began to ache with the effort of staying still.

And then finally, as the last rays of sun dipped behind the field, my necklace caught the light and reflected it straight back into the unicorn's inky eyes. The air around us shimmered and glimmered, like stardust falling from the sky, and he walked towards me, as if that was the sign he'd been waiting for all along.

I reached up to stroke his velvet-soft nose, running

my hands through his messy mane. He had an earthy smell, like a barn full of damp hay. There was something familiar about it. I leaned into him and he edged even closer. His breath was warm on my hands. It made me smile. Granny Rae's charm had made this happen. It was magic. I was sure of it.

We stood close together like that until the sun disappeared completely, covering the field in shadows. I wanted to stay longer but it was getting dark and Mum and Dad might be worried. The unicorn pawed the ground and turned to go himself. His mother was probably waiting for him somewhere too.

The kitchen was empty when I slipped back in. Mum was bathing Boo. I could hear them as I went upstairs. She was singing *row, row, row the boat* while Boo squealed and splashed the water. I couldn't believe they were doing something so normal. I tried to imagine Mum's face if I ran into the bathroom and said 'I've just seen a unicorn in the field'. She'd probably laugh, or roll her eyes, and then turn straight back to Boo.

It was quiet at dinner. Trish sat there giving Dad the worst death stares while he attempted to coax her into a better mood, asking her about college and revision and her plans for the following weekend, as if the shouting and swearing had never happened – as if Trish hadn't sworn right in his face.

I stared down at the mound of peas on my plate.

Mum still insists on giving them to me even though she knows how much I hate them. I rearranged the whole lot to spell UNICORN and turned my plate round to show her. She was pushing her own peas around in small circles, her eyes fixed on Boo's monitor, watching the little red lights. I didn't actually see her eat a single thing the whole meal.

Finally, when Trish had made some excuse to get out of clearing up and Dad was busy soaking the plates, Mum asked me about my day. I'd just started to tell her about the cake sale and how I needed Granny Rae's Bakewell tart recipe when the lights on the monitor began to flash. She scraped back her chair and rushed out of the room.

Chapter Five

M y first thought when I woke up the next morning was that I must have dreamed the whole thing. I lay under my duvet trying to be rational. The unicorn charm was just a piece of jewellery passed onto me by Granny Rae. It wasn't magic. It didn't have special powers. And yet…the unicorn's velvet-soft nose…his messy mane…his warm breath on my hand.

I pulled my uniform on, grabbed my coat and slipped out of the kitchen door. If he *was* real, if it really did happen, I must've left a gap in the blackberry bushes climbing in to the field and then back again. I was almost too scared to look when I got down to the bottom of the garden, but the gap was still there. So were the scratches on my arm where I'd caught my cardigan on the fence.

It was stressful at breakfast. Boo was grisly and wouldn't take his bottle. He waved his arms about, batting it away, shaking his head. He's had problems feeding right from the start. His heart has to work much harder than normal babies and the effort of sucking makes him sweaty and out of breath. Sometimes it's such a struggle his face turns blue.

When he first came home from the hospital he had to be fed every two hours, night and day, on this special high-calorie formula. Dad made a chart to put on the fridge with a space for Boo's weight to be recorded at the end of each week. It was supposed to help Mum stay positive. To help her cope with the constant feeds and endless hospital visits.

She was trying all the usual tricks this morning – tapping Boo's lips with the end of the bottle, singing his favourite song, giving him a spoon to hold – but it only made things worse. He flung the spoon on the floor and began to scream, arching his back and thrashing his arms about like he was in pain.

"Maybe he's teething?" said Dad. "I'm sure I could feel a tooth coming through yesterday…"

"Even if he *is*, he still needs to eat!" Mum was almost in tears herself. She lifted Boo out of the high-chair and cuddled him close. "He can't afford to miss a whole feed. He's hardly had any!" She walked around for a bit until he was calmer and then handed him across to Dad.

"I'm going to get the thermometer," she said. "I think he's warm…"

I gulped my cereal down as fast as I could while they worried over my head. Neither of them noticed that I'd already been out or that I'd torn my cardigan.

It was one of those cold, bright days. I trailed down the lane to school in a daze. I'd seen a *real* unicorn. A real live unicorn had appeared in the field at the bottom of the garden and it wasn't a dream. I was so distracted I didn't see Belinda until she was standing right in front of me waving something in my face.

I thought it was another nasty note for a moment, but it was only my PE top. It must've dropped out of my bag, either that or she'd pulled it out on purpose without me realising.

"I was sure this must belong to someone in the *Infants*," she said, as if she was genuinely confused, "but it's got your name inside so it must be yours."

She held the t-shirt up above her head so I had to jump to reach it. "Come on, Ariella," she said. "I'm trying to give it back to you!"

I jumped as high as I could, snatched it back and stuffed it in my bag, my face burning. How many more jokes could she make about me being small for my age?

What was so funny about being short anyway? No one made jokes about her being tall.

She ran over to Faye, who had obviously watched the whole thing. And then I noticed something I'd never noticed before. Belinda's hair was really scruffy and knotted up at the back as if it hadn't been brushed for days. My hand went up to my own neat plaits. Even when Mum had been up for most of the night, she still found five minutes to do them.

There was no assembly on Tuesdays, so we did Circle Time instead. We moved all the desks to the side and made a circle with our chairs. We started with a game called Spells. Mr Major explained that each of us had the power to invent one new spell. We had to say what the spell was and why we'd invented it. If we couldn't think of anything when it got to our turn, we could pass.

There was lots of laughing and cheering as the 'talking shell' went around the circle. It was one of those shiny shells that you can press against your ear to hear the sea. Only the person holding it was allowed to speak.

Lucas Jamieson said he had invented a spell to make all teachers disappear so that children could run the school. Faye said her spell would make her hair naturally straight so she wouldn't have to spend ages straightening it every morning. Anisha was the first person to say something serious. She wanted a spell to make her granddad's cancer better.

I had no idea what to say when it got to my turn. No one knew about Boo, not even Miss Nightingale. It felt too private to talk about him anyway. I thought about saying my spell would be to bring Neve here, to Baywood Primary, but I was worried it might sound like I didn't want to make new friends. In the end, when the shell came to me I said pass.

When it got to Belinda she clutched hold of the shell with both hands and said she'd invented a spell that would help her find things that had gone missing. "What sort of things?" Mr Major asked. She reddened slightly. "Oh, you know, my front door key or my homework or my favourite top that I can never find when I want to wear it."

She passed the shell on quickly, her face still flushed. I wondered what she really wanted to find with her spell. It had to be something more important than a top. She turned suddenly and caught me staring. I looked away, but it was too late. I could feel her eyes burning into the side of my head. She was angry, and for some reason it was all directed at me.

I tried to avoid her at break, but she found me just before the bell. "*We've* made up a spell, haven't we, Faye?" She nudged Faye and Faye nodded. "It's a spell to make you grow. All you have to do is run around the playground three times and then do ten press-ups." The bell rang and

I walked away, their laughter following me all the way to the line.

It was double Art after lunch, my favourite subject, stretching across the whole afternoon. The only time all week when I didn't get into trouble for drawing and doodling in my books. And even better than that, it was Mr Major's planning time so Miss Nightingale was in charge.

She said we were going to make stained-glass dreamcatchers using coloured acetates and tissue paper. "We'll stick them on the windows when they're finished. They'll help brighten up the classroom during the gloomy winter months."

The first thing we had to do was design our picture on thick, black circular card. We could draw anything we liked, as simple or as intricate as we wanted, as long as it filled the space. I did a unicorn surrounded by rays of light. Each ray had a criss-cross pattern. It took me ages to get it right.

The next step was to use the picture to create a stencil. Miss Nightingale sat with me while I cut around my unicorn and then made a start on the rays. I wanted to tell her about Belinda. I tried out what I would say in my head. *Belinda's been mean to me. Belinda's been picking on me. Belinda's a bully.* Was she a bully? Would Miss Nightingale believe me? Or would she just say it was Belinda's idea of a joke?

At my old school they took bullying seriously.

There were friendship benches in the playground and a buddy system so you always had someone to go to if you were upset about something. There was a set of rules as well. If you broke one and someone told, you had to stand against the wall for two minutes or until a teacher said you could play again.

"I really love your design, Ariella," Miss Nightingale said as I snipped out the little pieces of black card to make the pattern in the rays. "And it's no surprise you decided to do a unicorn…"

I glanced up at her.

"Come on." She laughed. "Don't look so surprised. You've got a unicorn pencil case, unicorn rubbers, a unicorn keyring, unicorns all over your school bag. I'll have to start calling you Unicorn Girl at this rate!"

I breathed out, smiling to myself. I liked that. Unicorn Girl. I couldn't wait to go home and put on my necklace. My tummy flipped and dipped every time I thought about seeing the unicorn again, stroking his messy mane, watching him gallop around the field. I could picture him in my mind as clearly as the picture I was cutting out in front of me.

I'd just finished snipping out the last piece of card when Louise came over to see if there was any spare glue. "That's amazing, Ariella," she said. "I love it! I've done a butterfly but the pattern on the wings isn't symmetrical and it's come out all wrong!"

"Maybe Ariella could help you next time?" suggested Miss Nightingale. "She's got a really good eye for design."

My face heated up. I thought of all the things I could say to Louise, like *of course I'll help you*, or *I bet your butterfly is brilliant*, or *why don't I help you fix it right now?* Or *do you like unicorns?* By the time I'd unscrambled the words in my head she'd skipped off back to her own table.

Chapter Six

I don't remember ever being shy before we moved to Baywood. In my last report, Miss Owen actually said I was *too* chatty. These are all the things I loved the most:

1. Class assemblies, the more lines the better.
2. The end of year school play. I was one of the orphans in *Annie* and I even sang a solo.
3. Running for school council. I had to give a speech to the class about everything I would do to make things better and I only missed out by one vote.

4. Class debates – for *or* against, I didn't mind as long as I got to speak.
5. Showing new children and parents around the school.
6. Role-play in drama – especially when we did anything make-believe.
7. Talking to Neve. Talking and talking and talking. We talked so much Miss Owen had to move us in the end.

The house was empty when I got home. Mum had left a note in the kitchen to say Boo had developed a temperature and they'd taken him up to the hospital. Trish goes to netball on Tuesdays so she wasn't home either. I tried phoning Mum but it just rang and rang. Dad's phone went straight to voicemail. I thought back to breakfast and how Boo wouldn't take his bottle.

It was too quiet in the kitchen. I went upstairs to my room and put on my necklace. My hands shook slightly as I clasped it around my neck. Why wasn't Mum answering her phone? When would they be back? How high was Boo's temperature? Would he have to stay in hospital? How long would I be here by myself?

I stood at the window looking out at the field. The silence swelled. It filled my room, pressing into every corner. A minute passed, two minutes, three. I stared and stared until my eyes began to blur, until the bushes and the shrubs and the sky and the grass merged together, until finally, through the bare branches of the winter trees, the same flash of white.

I ran straight down this time, only stopping to grab a carrot out of the fridge. I had no idea if he'd eat it, but I couldn't think of anything else. It was wild and windy as I raced to the bottom of the garden. Crispy leaves danced in the air. The empty house disappeared behind me as I dived headlong into the bushes, scrambling up and over the fence.

He was in the exact same spot as the day before. His ears pricked up when he saw me. "Hello," I said softly, holding the carrot out in my open palm as he lolloped over. I thought he might be unsure about eating it, but he gobbled it down in one noisy gulp and then nibbled at my fingers as if he was hungry for more. I pulled my hand away, giggling. "I'll bring you another one tomorrow, I promise. There's loads in the fridge."

He raised his head, his nostrils quivering, and took off around the field. This time it was like he was showing off, performing for an audience, although he was still struggling to go in a straight line, veering one way and then the other, like a small boat caught in a storm. By the time he'd galloped all the way back to me he was blowing hard through his nose, his mane a tangled, scruffy mess.

I reached up to smooth it down, using my fingers to untangle some of the knots as carefully and gently as I could. As soon as I'd got it looking tidy, he tossed his head, messing it up again, a straggly tuft hanging down over one eye, as if to say, 'It's *my* mane, thank you very much, and this is the way I like it!'

I realised I didn't know much about unicorns at all, not *real* unicorns. They always looked the same in pictures – fully-grown and perfect, with pure white coats and spiral horns. But this unicorn wasn't in a picture. He was as real as me or Trish or Belinda Burns, and it was obvious that having a tidy mane wasn't important to him. The only other thing I knew about him for sure was that he liked carrots.

He gave another toss of his messy mane, walked around me in a tight circle and then lowered himself down, folding his legs neatly under his body. I blinked nervously. Was he having a rest, or did he actually expect me to climb on his back? He nudged my arm. My heart thudded. I'd ridden a pony before, but only with a saddle and reins and lots of help.

I shook my head. "I'm too small. Everyone knows I'm the smallest in the class."

He nudged me again, harder. There was something in his eyes. Something urgent, like he was trying to tell me something. "I can't," I said, still shaking my head. "I'm scared. I don't know how to ride. Not properly."

Granny Rae used to say it was important to do at least one thing that scares you every day. She said it when I was too frightened to swim without my armbands, when I swore I'd *never* swim without them. I remember her standing on the side of the pool, cheering me on. But this was different. Granny Rae wasn't here to save me now.

The unicorn let out a short, impatient whinny. What if he got fed up waiting? What if he gave up and went away and I never saw him again? I pushed my glasses up my nose, wiped my sweaty palms on my trousers and, before I could change my mind, I flung my leg across his back and pulled myself on, wrapping my arms carefully around his neck.

Chapter Seven

I couldn't help squealing as he stood up. It was like agreeing to go on a roller coaster at the fair and then wishing you could change your mind and get off again when it was too late. I clung on, gripping hold of his mane as the ground got further and further away.

"Look, Granny Rae!" I shouted. "I'm doing it! I'm doing it!"

I pictured her face breaking into a crinkly smile.

The unicorn took a few steps forward, and then a few more. I wobbled like a jelly but somehow managed to stay on. It was scary being so high up without any reins or stirrups. I had to concentrate hard, clenching every muscle in my body to stop myself from slipping.

He went slowly, one faltering step at a time, as if he was concentrating as hard as me, as if his spindly legs might give way at any moment. And then, just as I was starting to get used to it, he lurched forward suddenly, throwing me back. It was impossible to hold on. I tumbled off, landing with a thud in the grass behind him.

It took me a moment to catch my breath. My glasses were hanging off one ear and my trousers were splattered with mud. I wriggled my arms and legs to make sure nothing was broken and brushed myself down. The unicorn tossed his head, as if I was wasting time, folded his legs under his body and waited for me to climb back on.

I held my hands up. "No way! Look at me!"

He whinnied again, rolling his eyes, as if my mangled glasses and mucky trousers weren't important, as if giving up wasn't an option, as if this was something we *had* to do. "Alright, alright, I'll have another go. But I would appreciate a warning next time!"

I hopped and jumped and clambered on, wrapping my arms around his neck as he unfolded his legs to stand up. I managed to stay on a bit longer than the first attempt, until he did the lurching thing again. And again. And again. And each time I fell off, he whinnied and snorted and rolled his eyes until I climbed back on.

It took at least ten attempts to make it even halfway around the field. I'd never concentrated so hard, or for so long, in my life. Mr Major wouldn't believe it. The better I got at balancing, the better he got at going in a straight line, almost as if we were teaching each other. I laughed into the wind. It was crazy. I was in the middle of a field, learning how to ride a *real* unicorn.

Eventually, I managed to stay on all the way round. The unicorn dropped his head in relief, or maybe it was exhaustion. I nudged him gently with my knees, to let him know I was exhausted too. He seemed to understand. He walked back to where we'd started and stopped by the blackberry bushes so I could jump down.

"Thanks for the lesson," I said, stroking his velvet-soft nose. "I think I'm getting the hang of it. I promise I won't be so scared next time." I crossed my fingers tight. "If there *is* a next time."

I watched him as he trotted across the field towards the gate at the far end. I could see him as clearly as anything, but then at a certain point he wasn't there anymore, like when a magician waves his wand and makes something vanish.

"Bye," I whispered, my fingers still crossed. "See you soon."

Trish was in the kitchen, phone in one hand, a slice of toast in the other. "What on *earth* have you been doing?" she said as I came in. "You look as if you've been dragged through a hedge backwards."

I pulled at a loose thread on my cardigan where it was torn. She wasn't far off the truth. I had been through the hedge and back again, but I wasn't about to tell her why. She wouldn't believe me even if I did.

"Have you spoken to Mum and Dad?"

"They had to take Boo to the specialist heart hospital in London," she said. "They've seen the consultant and they're on their way home now."

My tummy twisted. "Is it serious?"

She shrugged. "No idea. Dad sounded stressed, but then when doesn't he?"

Sometimes I wondered if Trish cared about Boo at all. She wasn't even excited when she found out Mum was pregnant. She just made a face and said it was embarrassing, that Mum was too old to have another baby. I poured myself a glass of milk, grabbed an apple out of the fruit bowl and went upstairs.

My new room isn't anything like my old room. It's big and draughty with rattling windows and dusty floorboards. Dad hasn't painted it yet, so none of my pictures or posters are up, and the walls are a horrible mustard-yellow – the exact same colour as one of Boo's poos.

I decided to unpack the last few boxes still stacked up by my wardrobe while I waited for Mum and Dad to get back from the hospital. The first box had all my summer clothes in: shorts and t-shirts and an old pair of sandals.

It was hard to imagine the weather ever being warm enough to wear them.

There was a box of games – Operation, Jenga, Guess Who? and Kerplunk – and a box of old books. I spent ages sorting through them, remembering the best bits, putting a few of my favourites on my bedside table to read again.

In the very last box I found the present Neve gave me before we moved. It was a blank book with the words 'Sketch That Thought!' printed across the front. I sat on my bed and drew everything that had happened since Granny Rae's funeral – like a cartoon strip with speech bubbles and captions. I even did a picture of me holding Boo with his stinky nappy, desperately trying to remember the mysterious Russian words Uncle Boris had said before he left.

When I got to the bit about the unicorn appearing in the field for the first time, I decided to give him a name. I scribbled down a few ideas in the back of the sketch book: Snowy, Sparkle, Starlight. I even thought of Ghost. But in the end, I decided to call him Albert. Well, I didn't *decide* exactly, I just found myself adding Albert to the list even though the thought had never actually entered my head.

It was a funny name for a unicorn. I had absolutely no idea where it had come from, but once I'd said it out loud a few times, it seemed like the best fit. Ariella and

Albert. Albert and Ariella. Either way round it sounded like we were a team.

It was late by the time Mum and Dad got home. Boo was fast asleep in his car seat. His face was flushed and his hair was stuck to his head as if he'd been sweating. The doctor at the local hospital had sent them straight to the specialist hospital, and eventually, after lots of tests, they diagnosed an infection and put him on antibiotics.

"I don't think I've ever been this exhausted," said Mum sinking down on the couch. "Not even those first weeks after Boo was born. I am honestly *so* sick of hospitals…"

"But what about his heart? Did he have a scan? Has the hole got any smaller?"

Mum shook her head. "He has to go back for a scan in a week or two, when the antibiotics have had a chance to work. They said the infection was affecting his appetite, and if he carries on losing weight…"

She didn't need to finish her sentence. If Boo lost any more weight they'd definitely have to operate. It's called 'open heart surgery'. I'd looked it up on the laptop. They would cut right through Boo's chest bone, open the chest cavity and connect his heart to a special pump called a bypass machine. The bypass machine would then take over the function of his heart while they repaired the hole.

They would literally stop Boo's heart beating.

I remember once we broke down on the motorway. When the recovery van arrived to rescue us, the mechanic tried to get the car going again. He used these long leads and bright orange clips and a special gadget called a multimeter, but nothing worked. In the end he stood there, scratching his head, and said, "That battery is as dead as a dodo!"

Would fixing Boo's heart be like that? Would they struggle to get it going again once they'd repaired the hole? Would *he* end up dead as a dodo? I pushed the thought away and went into the kitchen to make Mum a cup of tea. By the time the kettle had boiled and I went back in she was already asleep, slumped on the couch still wearing her coat.

I left the tea on the table and went upstairs to find Dad. He was settling Boo in his cot. He held his finger to his lips when he saw me hovering on the landing and crept out, gently closing the door. I leaned in to him and he pulled me close, stroking my hair. I could hear his heart beating through his shirt. Strong and steady. Ba-boom. Ba-boom. Ba-boom.

Chapter Eight

The infection dragged on. Boo slept loads more than usual, and even when he was awake he was grizzly and bad-tempered. I rushed home from school every day, but it was difficult to get a smile out of him, even when we read *Ricky the Rocking Horse*. Mum was so tired herself she was like a zombie-mum. I don't think she knew I was there most of the time.

Our neighbour, Sheila, came over a few times. She lives a couple of houses down from us. She's got a three-year-old, Maisy, and a baby called Ruby. She wanted to know if Mum fancied a walk or a cup of coffee, but Mum wouldn't even go to the door. She made Dad say she was having a rest, or that she was busy with Boo.

If Boo was sleeping when I got home from school, I'd go straight up to my room and wait at the window for Albert. Sometimes he appeared as soon as I put on my necklace, other times it took longer, but the moment I saw the familiar flash of white through the trees I'd grab my coat, smuggle some carrots out of the fridge and rush down to the field.

He always gobbled his carrots up first and then nuzzled in close for me to stroke his mane. I always attempted to smooth it down, and he always waited until I'd finished before tossing his head so that the same scruffy tuft flopped down over one eye. And then, after carrots and cuddles, we'd set off, wibbling and wobbling our way around the field.

The longer we spent together, the closer we grew. I loved the way he did an excited 'trot on the spot' welcome as I climbed over the fence, and the way he nibbled my fingers when he'd finished his carrots. I looked forward to seeing him all day and dreamed about him at night.

Mum and Dad were far too worried about Boo to notice I was outside for hours at a time, and Trish wouldn't look up from her phone even if I rode Albert straight through her bedroom. I didn't tell anyone, and the secret burned inside me, keeping me warm like a mug of hot chocolate on a freezing cold day.

It was the cake sale on Friday. Belinda had gone on and on all week about the amazing homemade cheesecake with fresh strawberries she was going to bring in. I'd been planning to make Granny Rae's Bakewell tart on Thursday after school, but then Mum thought Dad was getting the ingredients, and Dad thought Mum was getting them, and in the end I had to buy a packet of plain muffins at the local shop.

I spotted Belinda as soon as I walked into the playground. It would be difficult to miss her. She had a crowd of girls around her and she was showing them something. Faye was standing off to the side, watching. Her hands were curled into fists and her face was flushed, as if she was getting ready to hit someone.

When the bell rang and everyone ran to line up, I saw that Belinda was holding a plate with a big chocolate cake on it, covered with glossy chocolate icing. She walked to the line with the plate held out in front of her, like she was presenting the Crown Jewels, just to make doubly sure everyone could see how brilliant it was.

"No cheesecake, Belinda?" said Mr Major as we came trailing into the classroom.

"My mum thought it might go off, being out of the fridge all day," she said quickly, "so we made a chocolate cake instead." Her face flushed as red as Faye's. "At least it's homemade," she added, nodding at my packet of muffins. "At least *I* made the effort." At which point Faye gave a little yelp and ran out of the classroom saying she needed the loo.

It didn't take a master detective to work out that it was actually Faye who had made the chocolate cake and that Belinda was pretending it was hers so she could take all the credit. Mr Major didn't seem to have a clue. When Faye slipped back in halfway through Maths, all he did was tap his watch to let her know she'd spent too long out of the room.

At morning break there was a big argument in the playground. I wasn't close enough to hear the actual words but by the time we got back up to the classroom it seemed as though Belinda and Faye were friends again. And when it came to selling the cakes at the end of the day, Belinda sliced up the chocolate cake and said she would sell one half while Faye sold the other.

Mr Major noticed *that,* of course, and said it was extremely kind of Belinda to share her cake with Faye and that Faye was lucky to have such a good friend. I glanced across at Faye. Her face was frozen, her eyes bright with tears. I waited for her to say the cake was actually hers, but she didn't make a sound.

As soon as the sale started, Miss Nightingale came straight over and bought one of my muffins for 50p. "These look yummy, Ariella," she said, peeling the paper off and taking a bite.

I could tell she was just being nice. "I really wanted to make my Granny Rae's Bakewell tart, but there was a mix-up at home over who was getting the ingredients."

"Never mind," she said, taking another big bite. "Sometimes the simple things are the best!"

We carried on selling until every last cake, cookie and muffin had gone. Mr Major said he'd let us know how much we'd raised for our Winter Olympics on Monday, when the office had added it all up. I still had no idea what the Winter Olympics was. I had a sinking feeling it might be exactly the same as sports day, only in the winter instead of the summer.

As I was leaving school, I saw Belinda trailing down the lane towards Fallowfield Estate by herself. She usually walked home with Faye, but Faye was up ahead with Melanie Sykes, their heads close together, giggling about something. It was the first time I'd ever seen Belinda on her own.

Chapter Nine

I was still thinking about Belinda when I got home. You'd have to be desperate to take someone's cake and pretend it was yours. And what happened to the *amazing* homemade cheesecake with fresh strawberries? Why brag about it all week and then turn up empty-handed? It didn't make sense.

I let myself in with my key. The house was empty again. Dad had gone to see someone about a possible decorating job, his first since Boo was born. I had no idea where Mum was. She hadn't left a note or anything. I tried phoning her but it went straight to voicemail.

I still wasn't used to being in the house by myself,

especially when it was so cold and gloomy out. I grabbed a few carrots and trailed upstairs to my room. Luckily it only took a few moments for Albert to appear. A few moments of wishing and praying and peering across the lawn, through the bare branches and into the empty field. I banged on the glass to let him know I was on my way, and then rushed back down and out into the garden.

We went through our usual routine: his funny 'trot on the spot' welcome, a couple of carrots, a quick cuddle and then once round the field – this time with no sudden lurches or embarrassing falls.

"We're getting pretty good at this, Albert," I said, scratching the space between his ears. "I bet we could speed up a bit now that we've got so good at walking."

The second the words were out of my mouth he let out an excited whinny and began to trot, almost as though he'd been waiting for me to give him permission. And then just as I'd got used to the new rhythm, telling myself that trotting was exactly the same as walking, only faster, he sped up again, quickly going from a trot to a canter.

"Hang on," I wailed, "I'm not ready! I know I said faster, but I didn't mean *this* fast!"

I held on as tightly as I could. Cantering around the field with no saddle or reins was completely different from walking or even trotting. How on earth was Albert so confident all of a sudden when only a week earlier he'd been struggling to walk in a straight line?

I think we'd gone all the way around the field twice before I properly opened my eyes and another couple of times before I dared loosen my grip. I couldn't believe how fast we were going. It was like the scene in *Mary Poppins* where the carousel horses break loose and take off across the park.

"I think I like walking better!" I shouted, my voice bouncing up and down like a ball. But even as I struggled to stay on, focusing like I'd never focused before in my life, I realised I was doing okay. Albert wasn't the only one who'd grown in confidence. He ignored me anyway, determined to show off his new skills.

He must have been practising in secret when I wasn't there. I had no idea where he went or what he did in between the time we spent together. Or maybe he'd pretended to find walking difficult just to wind me up. He was definitely cheeky enough. I could just imagine him whinnying to himself every time I fell off.

I started to smile at the thought of him tricking me, and then I laughed out loud. "This is amaaaazing, Albert!" I shouted. "This is soooo amaaaazing." My heart pounded with excitement as we flew around the field, the world rushing by in a muddy blur. Ariella Bold – greatest bareback rider of all time!

It didn't take long before I needed a break. I nudged Albert with my knees to let him know I'd had enough, expecting him to slow down to a trot and then a walk, but with no warning at all he stuck his front legs out, screeching to a halt like when a car does an emergency stop.

It was impossible to stay on. I flew straight over his head, landing in the grass with a clumsy thud. I was so shocked I just sat there trying to work out what had happened. My glasses were lying in front of me. I fumbled around for them, hoping I could twist them back into shape, not feeling quite so 'great' anymore.

Albert was standing with his head down, shaking it slowly from side to side as if he was majorly embarrassed about the whole thing. "Brilliant cantering," I said, pushing my mangled glasses up my nose as he trotted over. "But maybe next time you could try slowing down before you stop!"

I could see Mum, Boo and Trish in the kitchen as I came up the garden. Boo was sitting in his highchair and Mum was trying to feed him some kind of bright orange mush. I burst through the door, out of breath and covered in grass.

"There you are," said Mum. "Sorry I wasn't in when you got home. I'd run out of Boo's special formula and…" She glanced up and literally dropped the spoon. "What on earth have you been doing, Ariella? I don't mind you spending so much time outdoors, but look at the state of you – you're filthy! And *please* don't tell me you've broken your glasses!"

Trish snorted. "Seriously, it's so sad. Haven't you got anything better to do?"

"There's nothing *wrong* with playing in the garden," said Mum, giving Trish a look.

"*Playing?*" said Trish, as if it was the most stupid thing she'd ever heard. "*In Year 6!*"

I was itching to tell her what I'd really been doing, but what was the point? She'd only think I was even more pathetic, making up stories about secret unicorns and cantering around the field. Granny Rae was the only person who would believe me. I gave Boo a quick kiss and went upstairs to draw everything in my sketchbook, including Albert's emergency stop!

It was just the four of us at dinner. Boo was already asleep. Dad's work meeting had gone well and he'd opened a bottle of wine to celebrate. It was for a job in the next village, decorating the upstairs of a massive house. I loved hearing about Dad's work. He always had funny stories to tell.

There was this one lady who used to put out a plate of homemade shortbread and then watch over him until he'd eaten every last piece. By the end of the job he'd put on three kilos. And there was this other time he was decorating a house and the little girl who lived there got her head stuck between the bars of the bed and they had to call the fire brigade to cut her free.

He was in the middle of telling us about the family

he'd met with today, and their mad, yappy dog, when Mum began to shake her head.

"I'm sorry, David," she said. "I've changed my mind. I don't want you to do it."

Dad let out a long breath. "Come on, Mandy. You said you were ready for me to go back. We decided. It's been over eight months."

"I know, but that was before the infection. What if I'm here on my own with Boo and something happens? What if he's really poorly? Or stops breathing? You do realise he could just stop breathing!"

It wasn't the first time Mum had freaked out about Dad going back to work. "Look, I won't be far," Dad said tightly, "and you can always call on Sheila. She's only two doors down. You said yourself she's home most days with the baby. I can't afford any more time off. You know I can't! The bills are piling up and—"

"*Bills?*" snapped Mum. "Please don't talk to me about the bills when Boo's health is at stake. And don't talk to me about Sheila either. I can't rely on her to help. She's basically a stranger. I don't even know her."

"Well, maybe you *should* get to know her. She's our neighbour and she seems really—"

"For Christ's sake!" Mum slammed her hands down on the table before he could finish. "Stop hassling me. And stop going on about Sheila. I'm sick of it. All I'm saying is, I don't want you to go back to work until Boo's had his scan and we've got the results and we know what's going on. Is that really so unreasonable?"

"When is the scan?" asked Trish.

"What do you mean *when is the scan?*" Mum looked at Trish as if she couldn't believe she was even asking. "It's tomorrow. You know it is. At least you would if you took the slightest interest in your brother. And I want you to stay in with Ariella. We don't know how long we'll be at the hospital. It could be hours and she'll be here on her own."

"Sorry," said Trish, waving her fork at Mum. "I can't stay in, not tomorrow. I've got plans. You can't just expect me to be free on a Saturday without giving me any notice!"

"Without giving you *what?* Is that supposed to be some kind of sick joke?"

I thought Mum was going to hit her. I shrank back in my chair.

"Calm down, Mandy," warned Dad.

"*Calm down?*" She whipped back round to Trish. "We're talking about your baby brother going for a scan to see if he needs *major heart surgery* and you expect me to give you *notice?* I can't believe how *selfish* you are. I can't believe—"

"I'm *not* selfish!" screamed Trish. She burst out crying. "I didn't know you wanted me to babysit. I'm not a mind reader! I can't help it if I've got a life!" She scraped back her chair and stumbled out of the kitchen.

"Trish!" shouted Mum, and then burst out crying herself.

"I'll just come with you to the hospital," I said. "I don't mind, honestly."

As soon as I said it, I wanted to take it back. I did mind. I hated hospitals, especially since Granny Rae died. I hated the smell, and how sad and grey everyone looked, and how sometimes the person you went to visit never came home again.

Chapter Ten

Saturday mornings used to be my special time with Mum. We had the same routine every week. She'd take me to my swimming lesson first (not my favourite part of the morning) then we'd go to the library so I could choose a pile of new books, and finally we'd go over to Granny Rae's for hot chocolate and iced buns.

What I remember most was how much we used to laugh. Like there was this one time we were in the changing rooms at the swimming pool. It was a few months before Boo was born and Mum was still squeezing into her normal jeans. She said she didn't want to waste money on expensive maternity clothes she was never going to need again.

Anyway, I was getting dressed after my lesson and suddenly the button on Mum's trousers pinged off and hit this woman on the back of her head and Mum said, "I'm so sorry. I seem to have put on a bit of weight recently," and the woman gave her this really funny look like she wasn't sure if Mum was joking or not, and Mum caught my eye and we started to laugh and once we started we couldn't stop. We laughed so much, Mum actually wet herself.

We set off for the hospital straight after breakfast. I sat in the back with Boo. He cried the whole way there, as if he knew where we were going. Mum leaned through from the front, singing his favourite song: *Horsey, horsey don't you stop, just let your feet go clippety-clop...* I sang along with her for a bit, but it didn't make any difference.

It felt like we were in the car for hours. The specialist heart hospital is nearer to our old house than where we live now. I stared out of the window. If I'd known where it was, I could've arranged to see Neve. Mum and Dad could've dropped me off on the way. I haven't seen her since we moved.

Boo finally fell asleep literally two minutes from the hospital. He'd worn himself out crying. His face was red and blotchy, and his nappy needed changing. We took the lift to the fifth floor and then walked down a maze of corridors to get to the right clinic. I trailed behind Mum and Dad. They'd been to the heart hospital loads of times, so they knew the way.

The clinic was in a lovely room, much nicer than I was expecting. The hospital where I visited Granny Rae was dark and gloomy, and it had this horrible, mouldy smell like old plimsolls. The children's heart clinic was bright and cheerful with huge cartoon animals painted on the walls, and pale, wintery sunlight streaming in through the windows.

One of the windows was stained glass, like the dreamcatcher I was making at school in Art. The glass had been painted orange and blue and red, throwing patches of colour across the floor. There were two wooden toy boxes, a big bookcase in the far corner stuffed full of books and comfy beanbags so you could sit and read.

Mum took Boo straight off to the toilets to change him while Dad and I queued up at the reception desk to let them know we'd arrived.

"The consultant doesn't usually keep us waiting long," said Dad. "You can stay in here if you like. The toys are a bit babyish, but you might find something good to read."

A young girl in the queue started moaning, pressing her hand into her side. However cheery the room was, it didn't change the fact that everyone there was sick.

I left Dad at the desk and trailed over to the bookcase, relieved I wouldn't have to go in with them. I couldn't bear to see Boo upset again, especially if he had to have an injection or a blood test.

There was a mixture of books. A few Harry Potters, a bunch of picture books, including some that Boo has at home, and at least four David Walliams. I've read all the Harry Potters already and I wasn't in the mood for anything funny.

I kneeled down and chose a few random paperbacks off the bottom shelf to flick through. When I went to replace them, I noticed a small, slim novel hidden behind the row of books, pushed flat against the back of the bookcase. I pulled it out carefully, running my hand over the cover.

It wasn't like the other books in the bookcase. It didn't say who the author was for a start, and there was no blurb on the back. It was very old, the pages furry and curled at the edges, and it had a musty, dusty smell, like when something's been packed away for a long time.

It was called *The Lost Unicorn*. Underneath the title there was a picture of a young, gangly unicorn with the saddest eyes I'd ever seen. I had the strangest feeling the book had been left there especially for me. That I was meant to find it. Like a sign. First Granny Rae leaving me her unicorn charm, then Albert appearing in the field, and now this.

I took it over to one of the beanbags, wondering how much time I had before Boo's appointment was over. I'm a fast reader, but even so, I wasn't sure I'd be able to read the whole book in one go. There was a prologue called 'Before the Beginning'. I smiled to myself. How could there be something *before* the beginning?

> Long ago, in far off times, unicorns roamed
> freely across the lands. These kind and noble
> creatures could be found in dense woodland,
> only leaving their homes to find and protect
> those most in need. Each unicorn was unique,

with its own features and personality.

Many people believed that if they were lucky enough to see a unicorn, they would be blessed with good fortune. The hungry would find food, the lonely would find friendship, and the poor would be rewarded.

However, over time, these harmless superstitions took on a sinister twist. A single sighting was no longer enough to satisfy some people. They wanted more than luck. They came to believe that the unicorn's horn was magic – that it could cure the sick, even those who were at death's door.

This put the unicorns in grave danger. Specialist hunters would track and kill them with a single arrow to the heart. Once caught and killed, the hunter would chop off the unicorn's horn and grind it into a fine powder. This powder would then be sold to the highest bidder.

Eventually, when only a few unicorns were left, a harsh winter swept the world. It was known as The Deep Freeze. The icy conditions and plummeting temperatures drove the surviving unicorns into hibernation. Easily camouflaged in the snow, they were finally safe from hunters.

The Deep Freeze lasted for many, many

years. The unicorns slept on safe under their snowy blanket. By the time the temperatures started to rise and the snow began to melt, no one had seen a unicorn for so long it was widely believed that they had become extinct.

Waking up from their endless sleep, the surviving unicorns found themselves in a world full of forests and fields and tall grassy hills. Taking no chances, they used the magic from their horns to weave an invisible barrier that would protect them from the evil hunters and their deadly arrows.

With spools of transparent twine wound tightly around their horns, they set to work, spinning and sewing and knitting and lacing – the fibrous thread leaving a faint spiral pattern on their once-smooth horns. They didn't stop until they had created a membrane that stretched from the forest floor to the tops of the trees, separating the human world from the unicorn world forever.

I wasn't sure if it was a fiction book or not. The way it was written, it sounded so real. Some of the words were tricky but I understood enough to get the meaning. I watched a nature programme once that said there had been at least five major ice ages in the past. Was The Deep

Freeze one of these? Had unicorns really hibernated in the snow until humans thought they were extinct?

I snuggled down further into the beanbag and turned to the first chapter.

The storm came with no warning. The skies had been clear for days, and then suddenly a darkness washed across the heavens, blotting out the sun. Afterwards, people said it was the worst storm they'd ever known. Trees were uprooted, flash floods swept through the village, houses lost their roofs.

But that wasn't the only damage caused by the storm. Deep in the darkest wood, a young unicorn foal bolted in fright. He'd never seen lightning before, never heard thunder. He thought it was the end of the world. Lost and confused, the unicorn foal ran for his life – through the woods, across the fields and up a steep hill.

As the storm raged around him, crashing and flashing, he ran higher and higher, right to the top of the hill, where he slammed into the invisible barrier, ripping the fabric with his horn. Tumbling through the trees on the other side, the unicorn foal landed with a thud on a soft bed of leaves below.

When he'd recovered enough to move again, he searched in vain for a way back. He wandered all that day, up and down the edge of the wood, pressing against the membrane, growing weaker with every hour that passed, unaware that the tear in the fabric was out of reach, high above his head.

A faint memory stirred. A story that Granny Rae used to tell me at bedtime. She never read to me from a book. Her stories always came straight from her imagination. I was only little, so it was difficult to remember the exact details, but I was almost certain there was one about a unicorn lost in the woods.

I was still reading when Dad came to find me to say the appointment was over. I blinked up at him surprised. I'd been reading for more than an hour. I was so absorbed in the story it was like coming out of a trance. The little unicorn was still lost, desperately searching for the tear in the invisible membrane. It was difficult to see how he was going to survive for much longer.

"Come on, love," said Dad. His voice was dull and heavy. I stood up, holding onto the book. I wanted to take it with me. I thought about asking one of the nurses, but it seemed mean, taking a book from a children's hospital. I decided to slip it back where I'd found it, hidden behind the row of books. Hopefully, if I came back, I'd be able to find it again.

Boo slept all the way home. Dad explained that he'd lost just over a kilo since the infection. The hospital would continue to monitor him and then scan his heart again in a couple of weeks. If he'd lost even more weight by then, they'd have to book him straight in for surgery. They were worried that Boo's condition was more complex than they first thought. They couldn't afford to take any chances.

Mum hardly said a word the whole way. She sat stiffly in her seat, shredding a damp tissue she was clutching until it lay in limp pieces all over her lap. I stared out of the window, thinking about the unicorn story. If this was thousands of years ago, a single sighting of a unicorn might be enough to help Boo.

Sheila from two doors down was walking past with her baby just as we arrived home. She stopped to say hello but Mum bolted from the car and rushed inside, leaving a trail of torn-up tissue behind her.

"Sorry about that," said Dad, getting out of the car. "We've just come from the hospital with Boo and it wasn't great news, I'm afraid."

Sheila's baby, Ruby, was sitting up in the pram, smiling, her cheeks plump and rosy red in the cold. She was only five months old, three months younger than Boo, but she was almost twice his size. I couldn't take my eyes off her. She was giant. I was so used to Boo, still small enough to fit into his baby clothes.

"It'll be alright," said Sheila, putting her hand on Dad's arm to reassure him. "He'll soon regain the weight. He's a fighter, you'll see."

Mum didn't come out of her room all evening. Dad made toasted cheese sandwiches for dinner with mugs of tinned tomato soup. It's the only thing he knows how to make. Trish arrived home just as we were finishing. Dad told her about the appointment and how much weight Boo had lost.

"He'll be alright," she said, barely glancing up from her phone, practically echoing Sheila. I didn't get it. How could she be so sure? Or did she just say the first thing that came into her head? Dad offered to make her a sandwich, but she said she had revision and went upstairs. I waited for her to slam her door, tensing my shoulders, but for once she closed it quietly.

Chapter Eleven

Sometimes it felt as if Sunday lasted twice as long as any other day in the week, especially since we moved to Baywood. Trish usually slept for most of the morning, while Mum and Dad took turns feeding Boo and catching up on sleep themselves. I was basically left to entertain myself, creeping around like a mouse until they were ready to start the day.

This Sunday something woke me early – it wasn't even six. I lay still in my bed, listening. Boo was crying. A horrible high-pitched wail. And over the wail, Mum's voice, soothing him. It wasn't his normal cry. I got out of bed and crept onto the landing. Mum was holding Boo.

He was limp in her arms. She turned her head and waved me away, mouthing that I should go back to sleep.

I stumbled into my room and over to the window, ducking under the curtains. I made a silent deal with myself. If Albert showed up, everything would be fine. Boo would be fine. That was the deal. I pressed my palms against the glass, closing my eyes. *Come on, Albert. Come on, Albert. Come on, Albert.* And when I dared take a peek there he was, galloping across the field, ears flat against his head, as if he'd heard my whispered prayer.

I don't think I'd ever got dressed so quickly. I grabbed a big handful of carrots and crept out of the kitchen door, closing it as quietly as I could behind me. It was cold and dark in the garden. A faint slither of moon hung in the sky. I zipped up my coat and skipped down to the bottom, hoisting myself over the fence.

"I'm here, Albert," I called. "I'm here!"

Albert was just as excited as me. He did his usual 'trot on the spot' but in a whizzy circle, going round and round at least three times before he came bounding over. As he stood close to me, gobbling down his carrots, I noticed he was losing some of his grey spots. They seemed to be fading as he grew taller, and his mane was definitely less tangled than when he first appeared in the field.

I reached up to touch the faint spiral pattern etched into his horn, remembering the unicorn story at the hospital and the spools of transparent thread.

"Look at you," I said softly. "Growing up so fast."

He immediately shook his head from side to side, spraying bits of chewed up carrot all over the place, as if to say, *Not THAT fast, thank you very much.* I started to laugh as his mane settled in a matted, scruffy clump, the usual tuft hanging over one eye. I smoothed it back down, picking out the bits of carrot.

It was brilliant to know we had all day if we needed it. When he'd finished eating, we rode around the field going from a walk to a trot to a canter. It was still difficult to stay balanced. I had to sit ramrod straight, clenching my stomach and holding onto his mane, trusting he wouldn't make any unexpected moves.

The more we practised, the better I got. I slowly loosened my grip until I barely needed to hold on at all. We rode faster and faster, both of us in the zone as we pounded round. I was concentrating so hard I didn't notice that at a certain point Albert had changed direction and was heading straight for the gate at the bottom of the field.

I grabbed back hold of his mane and leaned forward. "Slow down, Albert! We've only just learned to canter, we can't start jumping over gates. Albert! This isn't the Olympiiiiiiiics!" I clung on, terrified. *"Don't jump, Albert,"* I begged. *"Please!"* And then suddenly, without even attempting to slow down, he did the 'stopping thing' again, digging his front hooves into the muddy ground and skidding to a halt, centimetres from the gate.

I just about managed to stay on this time, but ended up hanging upside down like a monkey, my arms wrapped tight around his neck. "Very funny," I said, pulling myself back up to sitting. "Except I'm *not* laughing!"

He'd clearly mastered trotting and cantering but was absolutely *hopeless* at stopping. By the time I'd recovered enough to carry on, I realised he was waiting for me to jump down and open the gate. Riding around the field at the bottom of the garden was one thing – riding outside in the *real* world was completely different. There was always a chance someone might drive past or be out walking their dog, however deserted it was.

All my instincts were telling me I should keep

Albert a secret, but I wasn't sure he would turn back even if I wanted him to. We were on a short country lane with tall hedges on either side. As we approached the bottom I realised it was the lane that leads into Fallowfield, the estate where some of my class live, including Belinda.

We trotted on, the estate snaking out before us. Row upon row of identical houses pressed snugly together, each with its own tiny lawn. It was still early. Most of the houses were dark with their curtains drawn. We rode straight through and out the other side into a small wood. It was dense with fir trees, and clumps of wild mushrooms growing out of the mossy ground.

Albert's hooves were silent on the uneven surface as he weaved in and out of the trees. There was something magical about the wood in the morning mist, the sun just starting to peek through the branches. I wondered if this was where Albert came every time he left me in the field.

I half expected to see another unicorn or a whole family of unicorns emerging from behind a thicket of trees. I kept an eye out, but the only other creatures I spotted were some noisy wood pigeons and a sleepy hedgehog curled up in a spiky ball.

I soon found out that weaving in and out of the trees was much harder than riding in a straight line. There were fallen logs and low branches and it was difficult to see more than a few metres ahead. It reminded me of doing the obstacle race on sports day at my old school.

We weren't going fast but I had to predict the direction Albert would take seconds before he turned, leaning to balance myself, ducking the low branches and holding on tight when we stepped over logs. We changed direction so many times it was impossible to keep track of where we were. I had to trust that Albert would remember the way out.

I don't know how long we'd been riding when he suddenly stopped. His ears pricked up as if he'd heard something. He stood completely still, like someone had flipped a switch or put a spell on him. His nostrils quivered. He lifted his head, looking around. "What is it?" I said. Was someone there? "What's wrong, Albert?"

But then, just as suddenly, his head dropped, the spell broken, and he carried on through the trees and out of the woods.

The estate was beginning to wake up as we made our way home. Curtains were open and lights were on. I saw a man reading the newspaper, an old lady feeding her cat, three children crowded around a computer. One couple were sitting down to breakfast – cereal, toast and some kind of jam. I watched as the lady dropped small pieces of toast for her dog.

I wondered what would happen if she sensed we were there and looked up. It felt as if any minute someone was going to spot us, maybe even someone from school. I tried to urge Albert on, anxious to get back to the field, especially after his strange behaviour in the woods, but instead of speeding up he stopped.

"Come on," I said, nudging him with my knees. "This really isn't the best place to have a rest."

We were outside one of the more run-down houses on the estate. The paint was peeling off the window frames and there was a rusty bike in the garden with both wheels missing. There was something sad about the house, as if no one cared about it. It badly needed a fresh coat of paint and some colourful flowers planted in the garden to brighten it up.

I peered through the front window, curious. Why had Albert stopped there? I could just about make out two people. A girl who looked the same age as Trish, maybe a bit older, and a girl around my age. The older girl was waving her arms about, yelling at the younger girl. The younger girl was backed up against the wall as if she was trying to get away, her hands pressed over her ears.

I couldn't hear what the older girl was saying, but she looked super angry. Albert walked a bit closer just as the older girl whipped round suddenly. I shrank back, convinced she must've spotted us, but she grabbed her bag, turned to shout one more thing at the younger girl and came storming out of the house, slamming the door behind her.

It was too late to hide but she strode straight past us as if we weren't there. She was wearing thick makeup, smeared under her eyes as if she'd been crying, and had a phone pressed to her ear. A moment later she disappeared around the corner, an old khaki backpack slung over her shoulders.

I glanced back through the window, but I couldn't see the younger girl any more. I pushed my glasses up my nose and leaned forward, squinting to get a better view. She was still there, huddled in the corner with her back pressed against the wall and her knees folded up to her chest. And then, peering even closer, I realised it wasn't just any girl.

It was Belinda Burns.

The second I clocked who it was Albert began to move again, trotting along the road that led out of the estate. Did he want me to see her? Is that why he stopped there? Was he *showing* me? Or was it just a coincidence? And how come the older girl hadn't seen us? Were we invisible? I looked back over my shoulder, confused, wondering if I'd made a mistake.

It was almost impossible to think the girl cowering against the wall was the same brash, bullying Belinda I knew at school. And if it *was* Belinda, who was the girl shouting at her? And why was she so angry? I tried to remember if Belinda had ever talked about her family. She mostly showed off about all the amazing things she did at the weekends: riding lessons, gymnastics, trips to the theatre.

Riding back along the lane, thinking it through, I wasn't sure anymore that the girl *was* Belinda. It wasn't as if I'd seen her all that clearly. She was at the other end of the room, against the wall, practically out of sight. By the time I'd left Albert in the field, crept up the garden and slipped through the kitchen door, I was almost certain it had been someone else.

It took me a moment to realise Boo was still crying. He must've been crying through my whole adventure. Dad had taken over from Mum. I could hear him pacing up and down in the hall, talking in a low voice. I made myself a bowl of cereal and sat at the table waiting for someone come down.

Chapter Twelve

I was standing in my usual place in the playground the next morning when Belinda came marching over. She was with Melanie Sykes, their arms linked together. The same Melanie Sykes I'd seen walking home with Faye on Friday afternoon after the cake sale. I glanced around but there was no sign of Faye.

"How was your weekend, Ariella?" Belinda said, sneering. "Melanie and I had the best time at hers yesterday afternoon, didn't we, Melanie?" Melanie nodded like a puppet. "We made popcorn and watched a movie and then Melanie's cousin, Bev, gave us both a *proper* manicure."

They held their hands out to show me their neatly painted nails and then skipped off, laughing. I'd definitely made a mistake. There was no way it had been Belinda cowering against the wall in the run-down house on the estate yesterday. I couldn't imagine her allowing anyone to shout at her like that. She'd just shout back louder.

Belinda stayed glued to Melanie's side all morning. They lined up together for assembly, hung out together at break and sat next to each other at lunch. I noticed Faye trying to join in with them a few times, but Belinda soon made it obvious three was a crowd. It was amazing how she always got things just the way she wanted them.

In some ways it was the easiest morning I'd had since joining Baywood Primary. Belinda was so busy making sure Melanie was her new best friend that she left me alone. No teasing, no knocking into me, no nasty comments. For the first time in weeks I began to relax. But the feeling didn't last long.

That afternoon, we started a new topic: Our Local Area. The idea was to work with a partner to research a local business and then plan, design and promote a new business to open on Baywood High Street. Sometimes we're allowed to choose our own partners for Topic. This time Mr Major had already paired us up, and when he read through the names, I was with Belinda.

I thought it must be a mistake. I sat there praying he'd said the wrong name or mixed me up with someone else. But it wasn't a mistake. Belinda was my partner, and somehow Mr Major expected us to work together. And to rub salt into the wound, as Granny Rae used to say, he'd paired Melanie up with Faye.

Belinda was just as upset as me. "*I* wanted to be with Melanie!" she complained. "Why can't we choose our own partners? It's not fair!"

"*Fair?*" spluttered Mr Major, on the verge of a Major Meltdown. "Life *isn't* always fair, I'm afraid, Belinda. Now stop making a fuss and go and sit by Ariella so we can make a start."

I'd never heard him speak to Belinda so sharply. She trudged over to my desk, giving me the worst death stare ever. Why on earth would Mr Major put us together? Was it supposed to be a joke? I didn't even have Miss Nightingale to watch out for me. She was on a two-day first aid course.

There was a list of all the High Street businesses up on the whiteboard and an iPad for each pair. We had to choose a business, find out everything we could about it and prepare a report. And then when the reports were finished, we were going to go up to Baywood High Street to ask local people if there were any shops they thought the area needed.

"I'm working by myself," Belinda muttered, "so

don't even think about copying any of my ideas." She opened her topic book and made a big thing of covering the page with her arm, but then Mr Major said we should choose *one* business to research between us. "Only one of you needs to write down the information, but make sure you're both equally involved."

Belinda slammed her book closed and then just sat there as if she wasn't sure what to do next. Everyone else around us was busy looking things up on their iPads, writing and talking and planning. "So…um…what sort of business do you think we should do?" I said in the end, anxious to make a start. "A big one like the supermarket? Or something smaller like a charity shop or the fishmonger?"

"*The fishmonger?*" said Belinda as if I was completely stupid.

My face burned up. I opened the iPad and searched the café Dad goes to sometimes, The Coffee Club. Every now and then Belinda looked over at what I was writing, jabbing her finger at the screen at something she wanted me to add, and each time she did that I pushed my book across to her and she scribbled it down herself.

When Mr Major came over to see how we were getting on, he looked at our notes and said we'd made a good start. I stared up at him, desperately trying to communicate telepathically how unhappy I was, but he was clearly rubbish at mind reading.

"Great work, you two!" he said. "Keep it up!"

I couldn't wait to get out of the classroom at the end of the day. I made sure I was nowhere near Belinda as we spilled into the corridor, and managed to get down the stairs and past the toilets before she could even think about following me. There was no way I could work with her. It was like asking me to be partners with a killer shark or a poisonous snake.

Chapter Thirteen

I ran the whole way home. I didn't really think Belinda would follow me, she was too busy cosying up to Melanie, I just needed to get away from Baywood Primary and Mr Major and the whole stupid project. It was bitterly cold. The wind stung my face. I pounded down the lane wishing I could keep on running forever.

It didn't take me long to get back. Mum and Dad were in the kitchen. I could hear them discussing something as I let myself in. "I'm not imagining things," Mum was saying. "It's very strange. In fact it's an out-and-out mystery."

"What's that?" said Dad.

I hesitated by the kitchen door, flushed and out of breath. What was she talking about? The unicorn charm? Albert? *What if she'd found my sketch book?*

"Carrots!" she said. "I bought a whole bag of carrots on Saturday and then when I went to make Boo's lunch there were hardly any left. I had to wrap Boo up and pop out to get some more."

"*Carrots?*" said Dad. "That's the mystery? It's not exactly crime of the century. 'Hello? Police? Send an officer round straight away, someone has eaten all the carrots!'"

"Very funny," said Mum. "Of course it's not a crime. I just want to know who's been taking them. There's no way it could be Trish – she's chronically allergic to anything healthy – and Ariella has never liked carrots…"

"It *was* me," I said coming into the kitchen. "I took the carrots."

Mum whipped round to stare at me as if I'd grown an extra head.

"I like carrots now," I said defensively. "It's not exactly *crime of the century.*"

"Nice one!" said Dad, swooping over to high five me.

"But you've always hated carrots," said Mum. "Especially *raw* carrots."

"That was when I was little," I said. "I'm allowed to change, aren't I?"

"It's okay, Ariella, I'm not cross. Eat as many as you like. Have one now, if you like."

I fixed a smile on my face as Mum took a carrot out of the fridge. I noticed Boo's feeding chart was gone. The fridge door looked bare without it. I'd got used to checking his weight at the end of each week.

"Where's Boo?" I said, suddenly realising he wasn't there either.

Mum glanced at Dad. "He's having a quick nap. He tired himself out at lunch. It's nothing to worry about, he's fine."

She nodded at me while she was talking as if that made it true, except I knew it wasn't true. He was basically exhausted after every feed these days, struggling to take even a few ounces of milk.

She rinsed the carrot under the tap and handed it to me. "Ariella eating carrots," she said, shaking her head as I escaped upstairs. "Wonders will never cease!"

It was the longest conversation we'd had in ages and it was all a lie. I was lying about liking carrots and Mum was lying about Boo. I used to tell Mum everything before Boo was born. She knew if I was happy, or excited or worried or sad. If I'd had a bad dream or I had lines to learn for an assembly. Before Boo was born I would've come straight out of school and told her I'd been paired up with Belinda for the project.

I put on my unicorn charm and stood at the window, wishing I had someone to talk to. Neve promised we'd stay best friends when I told her we were moving. She said she'd come and visit or I could go and sleep over at hers. I'd love to tell her about Uncle Boris giving me the unicorn charm and Albert appearing in the field and how much I hated Belinda Burns.

I used to talk to Trish too, before she turned into the biggest cow, literally overnight. Even though there was six years between us, we still had fun together. I heard her arrive home from school, come stomping straight upstairs and slam her door.

She'd been in a mood ever since Dad began confiscating her phone at bedtime. He'd read something about teenagers checking their phones constantly during the night. The article recommended switching all devices off at least ninety minutes before lights-out to get the best sleep. Dad said she should be revising more and using her phone less anyway, now she's at college doing her A Levels.

He came racing up after her, furious she'd slammed her door, yelling at her for being selfish. Boo woke up crying, and Mum rushed up to resettle him. Trish came back out of her room and swore at Dad again, even worse than the last time. We'd become a big, shouty family with slamming doors and angry voices.

It was freezing in my room, but my palms felt hot and clammy against the window frame. I wiped them on my trousers. They were tingling, like an electric current was running through my fingers. My heart began to gallop in my chest. It was like the day I first saw Albert, the same panicky feeling. I clutched hold of my unicorn charm, whispering Albert's name over and over, desperate for Dad and Trish to stop arguing.

And far in the distance, through the trees and across the field, a streak of white.

It was easy enough to slip out unseen. I didn't even have to stop for a carrot – I already had the one Mum had given me. It had started to rain, but only a few spots. "Albert! Albert! Albert!" I called, all the way down the garden, leaving the shouting and crying and slamming and swearing far behind me.

He did his usual 'trot on the spot' as soon as he saw me, and then came straight over for his carrot. He ate slowly, nibbling at the edges as if he had all the time in the world. When he'd finished he butted me gently with his nose and moved closer so I could stroke his mane and tickle the spot between his ears.

I told him about my day. About Mr Major pairing me up with Belinda, and how mean she was, and how I didn't have any real friends at Baywood Primary. Once I started talking, I couldn't stop. There was so much to say. It was properly raining now but I didn't care. I told him about moving house, and leaving Neve, and missing Granny Rae, and Trish and her horrible moods and how it was nearly my birthday but everyone had forgotten.

And then I told him about Boo. About how having

a new baby brother had changed everything, but not in the way I thought it would when I first found out Mum was pregnant. I told him how quickly my excitement had turned to fear. How all I'd wanted was a baby brother to look after and keep safe. Albert pawed the ground and moved even closer.

I told him about the chart on the fridge. How Mum and Dad had taken it down as if they'd given up any hope of Boo putting on weight. How scared I was that he might not get better – that his heart might not be strong enough to survive the operation – and that Trish didn't seem to care at all. She just stomped around, slamming doors and causing big shouty rows.

It was only when I broke off to take a breath that I heard a sound behind me. I tensed up, listening. It was my name. Someone was coming down the garden calling my name. I spun round. It was Trish. She stuck her head through the blackberry bush and then climbed over the fence right into the field.

"Ariella! For God's sake! I've been calling you for ages! Didn't you hear me?"

I stared at her for a second and then spun back around. Albert was still there. He hadn't moved. I blushed to the roots of my hair, as if I'd been caught doing something I shouldn't.

"And who were you talking to?" said Trish, looking straight over my shoulder. "I heard you, so don't deny it.

You were saying something about me."

I shrugged, realising she couldn't see Albert, that he was completely invisible to her, just like that time I thought I saw Belinda on the estate.

"Anyway, Mum wants you to help with dinner."

"Why can't *you* help for once?" I said, finally finding my voice.

"Too much revision," said Trish airily. "What are you doing down here anyway? Apart from standing in the middle of an empty field in the pouring rain talking to yourself like a total weirdo?"

"Nothing," I said. Tears stung my eyes. Why was she *so* horrible?

"Come on, then. Hurry up. I'm getting soaked and Mum's waiting."

Chapter Fourteen

The hospital sent a letter with the date of Boo's next appointment. It was a week away. A week for him to put on weight. The more weight he put on, the more likely it was that the hole in his heart was closing by itself. He seemed to be responding to the antibiotics, his temperature was down, but he was still off his food.

On Sunday he finished all his lunch for the first time since he caught the infection. There was lots of clapping and cheering at the table, but then a few moments later he sicked it all up. Mum tried to feed him something else, some mashed-up spinach, but he turned his head from side to side, fussing and crying, his mouth clamped shut.

"Come on, Boo," she pleaded. "You love spinach. Come on, just a little bit." She prised his mouth open with the end of the spoon but he thrashed about, shooting his fist out and knocking the entire bowl onto the floor.

"*Oh my God!*" shrieked Trish, scraping her chair away from the table. "Look at my top! It's ruined!"

"Well don't just stand there!" Mum rounded on her. "Get a cloth. Help me clean it up. Do something useful for once in your life!"

"This is ridiculous," said Dad. "If Boo's losing weight, it's because his heart isn't mending. It's not because you're not feeding him enough. Forcing him to eat isn't going to help anyone."

"*Forcing* him?" hissed Mum. She pushed her face right into Dad's. "I suppose you'd rather he had a major operation instead! I suppose you'd rather—"

"Just stop!" Dad put his hands on her shoulders. "For goodness sake, Mandy, just listen for a minute. Forcing Boo to eat is *not* going to mend his heart. You've got it all the wrong way round. He'll put on weight when the hole in his heart closes up. And if he needs an operation to make that happen, there's nothing you or me or any of us can do to change that."

Mum shook Dad off and scooped Boo out of his highchair. He was whimpering, covered in spinach. "I'm sorry," she said, smothering him with kisses. Silent tears trickled down her face. "My poor baby. I'm so sorry."

It was actually a relief to go to school on Monday. Miss Nightingale was back from her first aid course and she sat next to me while Mr Major introduced a new Maths topic – fractions. He wrote some examples on the board, as a starter, and asked us to order them from smallest to biggest.

I copied the fractions into my book, trying to remember how to work them out. I glanced around the room. Everyone was busy scribbling away. I tried to imagine the whole class lined up, smallest to biggest. I'd probably be at one end and Belinda right at the other. Except a few of the boys had grown since September, and so had some of the girls.

I wasn't so sure Belinda would be tallest anymore. Alfie and George had just about overtaken her, and it looked as if Melanie might be taller too. And then I began to wonder if I was still the smallest. I'd been feeling taller myself these past few weeks, although it was so long since Mum or Dad had measured my height against the wall, I couldn't be sure.

It was my birthday at the end of the month. I was going to be eleven. We used to plan my birthday weeks in advance. Granny Rae would make the cake and Mum and I would sort out my party. Planning it together was half the fun. I wondered what would happen this year, whether anyone would even…

"Earth to Ariella," said Miss Nightingale, waving

her hand in front of my face. "Let's make a start on these fractions, shall we?"

By the time Maths was over, my brain was frazzled. I still had loads to do. Miss Nightingale sat with me at first break and helped me finish. I didn't mind. It was easier to stay in. Belinda was now superglued to Melanie. It was amazing how quickly she'd dropped Faye, even though it was Faye who was upset in the first place because of the cake.

I couldn't help feeling sorry for Faye. I was sure she'd only been mean to me to impress Belinda. She was on her own all through lunch, watching Belinda and Melanie from the other side of the playground. I tried to catch her eye and smile a few times, but when she noticed she turned away as if she was embarrassed.

We somehow ended up next to each other in the line when the bell rang, both of us at the back. I thought about what I could say to make her feel better. *Sorry you got dumped by Belinda. I know it was you who made the chocolate cake. Why do you want to be friends with her anyway? Do you believe in unicorns?* None of it sounded right.

We finished our dreamcatchers in Art. I stuck different coloured, overlapping acetates onto the back of the stencil and held it up to the window. The light shone through the rays, making a chequered rainbow across my desk. Miss Nightingale was so impressed she said

I should show it to Ms Gilmore.

When I got down to the office, Mrs Lacey, the school secretary, called me over to her desk. "Can you tell Mr Major that I've added up the takings and your cake sale raised £64.30 for the new sports equipment? He'll be ever so pleased." She glanced at my dreamcatcher. "Oh, I do love unicorns!" she said. "I know they're not real, but even so, there's something *so* magical about them…"

I smiled to myself. She didn't know what I knew.

It was parents' evening after school. Dad had gone to talk to Mr Major while Mum stayed home with Boo. I wondered what Mr Major would say about me. Too quiet? Too slow? Rubbish at Maths? I sat at the top of the stairs waiting for Dad to come back. Mum was in the kitchen waiting for him as well.

"She's really struggling," I heard Dad say to her once he'd arrived home. "Mr Major's worried that she's falling behind. He says she finds it difficult to concentrate and that she hasn't settled well socially either. She hasn't made any firm friends. They've been doing their best to support her, especially Miss Nightingale. They understand how tough things must be, with Boo so poorly and then losing her gran…"

It was quiet for ages after that. I had no idea they knew about Boo at school. Mum and Dad must've told them when I joined. I went further down the stairs, straining to hear. Mum was crying. "I honestly can't cope with anything else." Her voice cracked. "I know she's been spending a lot of time on her own in the garden, but I didn't realise she was on her own at school as well. She must be *so* lonely... Oh God, I just wish my mum was here. I can't do this without her. I miss her, Dave..."

"Of course you do," said Dad. His voice was soft and warm like a blanket. "We *all* do, especially Ariella. It's been a huge upheaval for her: moving house, losing her gran, Boo's condition. Why don't we organise something for her birthday at the end of term? Invite one or two girls over from her class..."

I trailed back to my room thinking about Belinda and how small she made me feel, and how much I missed Neve and all the made-up games we used to play. And how at my old school everyone would sing happy birthday in the language of the month. I didn't want to do anything for my birthday this year.

Not with the girls at Baywood Primary.

Not without Granny Rae.

Not with Boo so ill.

Chapter Fifteen

Each day that passed, Boo seemed to eat less. It was like when he first came home from hospital. Mum was back to feeding him every two hours, right through the night. She begged and pleaded and coaxed the milk into him. It didn't do any good. By the time his scan came around on Friday he hadn't gained a single gram.

Dad talked non-stop at breakfast, making silly jokes about how he'd gained all the weight Boo had lost. Mum shot him a look, but it was obvious he was just as scared as she was. My tummy started to hurt. I didn't want to go to school. I didn't want to wait all day to find out if Boo was going to be okay.

"Eat up, Ariella," said Dad, pushing my toast a bit closer. I pushed it away. "I don't feel well. I've got a tummy ache."

Dad glanced at Mum. "I'm sure you're fine," he said.

"I'm not." Tears filled my eyes and spilled over. "I'm not fine. It really hurts, and if I go to school and I'm sick no one will be at home to come and get me and I'll have to sit in the nurse's room all day."

Boo was already strapped into his car seat, a line of dribble trailing down his chin. He looked too small, like he'd shrunk, like Granny Rae the last time I saw her.

"I want to come with you. Please let me come. I'll help in the car. He likes it when I'm there. I'll sing to him if he gets upset…"

Mum rubbed her hands across her eyes. "I honestly don't have the energy for this today, Ariella. I don't want you making a fuss, or getting upset at the hospital. I mean it."

"I won't, I promise."

I grabbed a tissue to wipe my face and then ran upstairs to get changed out of my uniform. I decided to wear my unicorn charm. Uncle Boris said it would bring me luck when he gave it to me at Granny Rae's funeral, and we desperately needed some of that luck today.

Boo slept most of the way there. Mum and Dad talked quietly in the front. They said things I didn't understand like 'unhealthy pallor' and 'failure to thrive'.

I stared out of the window, picturing Albert in the field, wondering if he ever showed up when I was at school or out somewhere else.

Dad dropped us off outside the hospital and went to find parking. Boo woke up as soon as the car stopped. Mum put him in his pram and we took him up to the clinic in the lift. I stroked the hair off his face, leaning down to kiss him. "Do you think he knows where we are?" I said, but Mum didn't answer.

The clinic was busier than the last time, and noisy. Two children were chasing around with plastic swords dressed up as Peter Pan and Captain Hook. They looked far too healthy to be there. I glanced around wondering if they had a little brother or sister who was ill. Someone like Boo.

I waited until Dad came up from the car park and then trailed over to the bookcase. The unicorn book was still there, pressed flat against the back, exactly where I'd left it. The poorly children and grey, worried faces of their parents faded into the background as I sunk into a beanbag, flicking through the pages until I found my place.

Weak with hunger and exhaustion, the frightened unicorn curled up close to where he'd fallen and slept. He dreamed of his mother, of her soft, warm body and kind eyes. He dreamed she found him sleeping on the wrong side of the membrane and took him back home.

When he woke, night had fallen and the woods were dark. The moon slipped out from behind a cloud, illuminating, for a fleeting moment, the tear in the membrane. Glancing up, the unicorn spotted the tear and realised he had fallen from a considerable height. His spindly legs trembled beneath him. He couldn't imagine ever being big enough or strong enough to jump back through.

Wandering away from the woods in search of food, he found a clearing and some vegetables growing in the ground. Carrots, swedes and turnips. The swedes were tough and chewy and the turnips bitter, but the carrots were sweet and nourishing. They gave him strength. Enough strength to realise that if he was ever going to see his mother again, he would have to find the courage to do something about it.

He set about the task with dogged determination. He found a field close to the woods and began to work hard to build up his strength. At first, he struggled to walk in a straight line. He was clumsy and uncoordinated, his gangly legs and oversized hooves pulling in different directions. But he persevered.

During the day he would wander from the woods to exercise and eat, and at night he would return to sleep close to where he fell through the membrane. And as the days turned into weeks, he grew taller and his legs grew stronger and he began to believe that one day he would find his way back to his own world.

"Boo's had his scan." Dad's voice, tense and quiet. I looked up. I was on Chapter Ten, about halfway through. "We'll know the results later today. They're going to phone us as soon as they can."

I slipped the book back into the bookcase, determined to read the rest next time I came to the hospital. We got caught in terrible traffic on the way home. It took ages. Boo began to cry and once he started he wouldn't stop. Mum gave him a rice cake to suck on, and then a teething rattle, but he threw them both on the floor. He screamed so loud the veins stood out on his head like a road map.

I tried singing 'Horsey, Horsey' to distract him but he thrashed his arms about, accidentally catching hold of my necklace, and then gripping hold of it tight.

"Is this what you want?" I said gently. "Granny Rae's

magic charm? Will this stop you crying?" I took it off and dangled it in front of him, swinging the unicorn from side to side like a hypnotist trying to put someone into a trance. Boo followed the charm with his eyes, one way and then the other, back and forth, until eventually his screams turned to sobs and then to hiccups and finally his eyes closed and he fell asleep.

"Thank you," said Mum, almost in tears herself. "I honestly don't know how you did it, Ariella, but thank you."

The heart consultant called later that afternoon to discuss Boo's scan results. The hole in his heart hadn't closed up and there were further complications, something to do with the blood circulating around his body. They were going to operate sooner rather than later and a date would be sorted out. It wasn't an emergency, but Mum and Dad should bring him straight in if he developed a temperature again or if he was struggling to breathe.

It was the strangest evening. Dad suddenly decided he was going to sort out the dining room. He said it was time to look forwards. He dragged Granny Rae's bed and chest of drawers out to the shed and asked me to pack away the bedspread. The bed was heavy and awkward to move. Dad heaved and scraped it through the house, forcing it through the door. Mum didn't do anything to help, but she didn't stop him either.

Boo slept through the whole thing. I went in to check on him before bedtime. He was in his cot, snuggled up in his baby sleeping bag, his beany bear tucked under one arm. I watched his chest rise and fall with each breath. Rise and fall. Rise and fall. "Don't stop breathing," I whispered. "Whatever you do, don't stop breathing."

Chapter Sixteen

I was dreading school on Monday, even more than usual. It was the second stage of our project and we were going to the High Street to conduct a survey. I tried convincing Mum that my tummy was hurting again but she felt my head, muttered something about not being able to deal with one more thing, and bundled me out of the front door.

Mr Major got us to line up with our partners as soon as we came out of assembly, handing each of us a clipboard and pen. It takes roughly fifteen minutes to walk to the High Street. Belinda made sure we were right in front of Melanie and Faye in the line and then turned round to talk to Melanie the whole way there, deliberately ignoring Faye.

Faye laughed along with them, pretending she was part of the conversation, and they were including her, even though it was obvious they weren't. I was dying to tell Faye, *and* Melanie, that Belinda wasn't a proper friend, but I kept my eyes down, wishing I was back at my old school with Neve.

Once we arrived, we were allocated a specific place to stand. Belinda and I were a little way down from the supermarket, outside a charity shop. Miss Nightingale said it was up to us to approach people and ask the questions, but she would hover nearby in case we needed any help.

It was a busy morning. People streamed past, mostly headed towards the supermarket. No one looked as if they had the time to chat. Belinda was brave enough to stop someone first.

"Excuse me," she said, going up to a lady with two small children. "I go to Baywood Primary and I'm doing a survey. Could I just ask you which shops you use the most?"

The lady said she was sorry but they were on their way to the doctor's, and she rushed off, dragging the children behind her.

"Don't worry, Belinda," said Miss Nightingale coming over. "Not everyone will have time to stop. Try not to be discouraged."

The next people Belinda went up to were much friendlier. They were an older couple. They said they used the supermarket and the chemist, and they bought fresh fish every Friday. They were in the middle of explaining how inconvenient it was that the local post office had closed down when Belinda froze.

It was like someone had pressed pause on the TV remote. Her face flushed bright red and a moment later, without offering any explanation to the couple she was talking to, she backed away from them and slipped behind me.

"Don't move," she hissed. "Whatever you do, stay *exactly* where you are."

The couple looked confused. The woman took a step towards us and then shrugged and turned away.

"How rude," she said sharply, taking her husband's arm. "Don't they teach you any manners at your school?"

I twisted round to see who Belinda was hiding from. A girl with thick makeup and an old khaki backpack walked past us. She had a phone pressed to her ear and she was talking very fast. It was the same girl I'd seen on the estate that night, the girl who'd stormed out of the house. Close up and in bright daylight, she looked like an older version of Belinda – but not that much older. They were almost identical.

The girl carried on down the road and disappeared into the supermarket. Belinda stayed where she was for another ten seconds or so and then stepped away from me. I waited for her to explain but she held her clipboard up, scribbling away as if she had something vitally important to write down.

"So who was that?" I said in the end. "Is she your sister?"

She turned away from me as if I hadn't spoken and went marching over to a woman in a smart suit, plastering a smile on her face and asking if she maybe had time to answer a few simple questions.

I had no way of knowing whether the girl *was* Belinda's sister, but Belinda's reaction to seeing her did make one thing clear. It was definitely Belinda I saw that morning on the estate. She was the girl cowering in the corner of the living room with her hands over her ears.

Eventually I plucked up the courage to stop someone myself – an old lady who reminded me of Granny Rae. She was tall and elegant, wearing a bright blue coat and a hat with a peacock feather sticking out of the side. She told me she was on the way to the supermarket and after that she was going to pop into the newsagent to buy a scratch card.

"I'm wearing my lucky hat, so you never know," she said, winking. "Someone's got to win, after all."

She answered my questions, and then as she carried on down the road someone else tapped me on the shoulder from behind. "It's Ariella, isn't it?"

I turned round. It was Sheila from two doors down. She had Ruby in the pram.

"We can do your survey, if you like. Maisy's at nursery so we're not in a hurry, are we, Rubes?" I stared at Ruby, my heart thudding. She was the healthiest-looking baby I'd ever seen. It was difficult to imagine Boo's cheeks ever being that plump and rosy, his eyes so sparkly and bright.

I dragged my eyes back to Sheila. I asked her what shops she used and if she thought the High Street was missing anything in particular. She said she was in and out of the chemist all the time and her hairdresser was across the road, opposite. I ticked the box next to chemist on my sheet and searched down the list of shops for the hairdresser.

"How's your little brother?" said Sheila. "I haven't seen your mum the last few days."

"He's got to have an operation," I said and then clamped my lips shut wishing I'd kept quiet in case Mum didn't want her to know.

Sheila leaned over the clipboard and pointed at the hairdresser down at the bottom of the list.

"I see you sometimes, Ariella. Playing out in my field."

I stopped mid-tick, my face heating up. "*Your* field? I'm sorry... I mean, I didn't know. I had no idea..."

"Oh, don't worry. Honestly. It's not a problem. You can play in there whenever you like, although it's a bit muddy at the moment, with all the rain we've been having."

I stared after her as she pushed Ruby down the road towards the supermarket. I couldn't believe the field at the bottom of the garden belonged to Sheila and that she'd actually seen me in there. I'd got so used to thinking of it as mine. Mine and Albert's.

I stopped a few more people, old ladies mostly, and then Miss Nightingale took us up the road to meet the others and we trailed back to school. Belinda didn't say a word the whole way. I still couldn't match her with the girl I saw cowering against the wall. It was as though they were two different people.

She didn't mention it again until the end of the day when school was over. I was trailing down the lane that leads home when she slipped out from behind a hedge, blocking my way.

"Don't tell *anyone* what happened today on the High Street," she said, grabbing me and yanking me towards her. Her fingers dug into my arm, right through my coat. She must have rushed ahead when the bell rang and then waited for me to walk past.

I shook myself free, staring at her.

"What, you mean when you saw your sister?"

"Just don't say anything." She looked down, her

eyes blurred with tears. "I mean it, Ariella. You'll be sorry if you do."

I was so surprised, I couldn't say anything for a minute. I'd never seen Belinda upset before, apart from when she'd been paired up with me on the project. She turned to go towards the estate, swinging her school bag over her shoulder just like her sister.

"I've got an older sister too," I called after her. "I don't get on with her either."

Chapter Seventeen

Dad says the first few days after Boo was born he hardly made a sound. He would hold Boo in his arms and Boo would stare up at him, pale and silent. "I kept saying 'boo!'– not to frighten him, obviously, just to see if I could get a reaction. You know, like peek-a-boo!" He says he wasn't used to such a quiet baby, not after me, and especially not after Trish.

Boo's real name is George but most people don't know. The only time I've ever heard anyone use it is when we're at the hospital and the consultant calls him for his appointment.

*

The letter with the date for Boo's operation arrived on Wednesday. I heard Mum on the phone when I got in from school. She was talking to her friend Lisa. She was telling her how awful it was, but that there was nothing they could do. That the operation had been scheduled for three weeks' time on December 10th.

I shook my head. *No, no, no. Not December 10th.* But she said it again. And then I heard her say delaying the operation or changing the date wasn't an option. I held onto the banisters, feeling sick. They couldn't operate on December 10th. They couldn't cut Boo's chest open and stop his heart on the same day as my birthday.

I shrugged my coat back on, tore through the kitchen and out of the door. Mum called after me but I ignored her. I stumbled down the garden without looking back. It was freezing cold. The sky was heavy. It pressed down on me as I climbed over the fence. *Not on my birthday. Not on my birthday. Don't let anything bad happen to Boo on my birthday.*

The field was empty. I closed my eyes and wished for Albert. I wished with everything inside me. My chest was tight. It was difficult to breathe. I counted to ten in my head and then opened my eyes again. Peering into the distance, I could just about make out the shape of him coming down the lane from the estate. The gate at the far end of the field was open and he galloped towards me, his tail swishing behind him.

I ran to meet him, calling his name. "No carrots today," I said as he pushed his nose into my hand, nibbling my fingers. "There wasn't time." He seemed to sense my mood, sense that I needed to get away. As soon as I'd mounted him and got my balance, he took off across the field.

We rode through the estate and into the woods. The sky darkened and it began to rain. I pulled my hood down tight. The wind was icy. It whistled through my ears. Albert wove in and out of the trees, picking up pace as if he was in a hurry, until we were right up against the fence that runs around the edge of the wood.

He was agitated, lurching one way and then the other, bucking his legs, blowing hard through his nose. I held on tight, scared for the first time in ages that he might throw me. He'd never behaved like this before. He ran up and down a few more times, and then stopped, threw back his head and let out an agonising cry.

I wrapped my arms around his neck. I could feel him trembling beneath me. He let out another cry, and then another, pausing between each one, almost as if he was expecting a reply. "What is it? What's wrong?" I strained to see through the trees as he flung himself around, his head down like a bull.

The sky lit up, followed by a loud crash. Thunder. The rain came down harder. "We need to get back!"

I shouted. "We need to go!" But he wasn't listening. He rode towards the fence and then backed up and then rode towards it again. I was soaked through and frightened. The wind tore round us, whipping him into a frenzy. I held on tight as Albert flung himself at the fence again and again and again.

The sky lit up once more, and Albert let out another terrible cry. For a fleeting second, I thought I saw something beyond the trees, something that didn't make sense – shadowy shapes, blurred movement. And then nothing.

He was trembling all over now, his head swinging like a giant pendulum. Rain ran down my face. I could barely see. "We've got to go," I pleaded. "We've got to go back." He let out one last cry, wailing with the wind, and then just as suddenly as it had all started, it stopped.

"Come on," I said, and he turned away from the fence and led me out through the trees.

We walked slowly, both of us exhausted. I kept seeing those shadowy shapes in my mind, as Albert's anguished cries echoed around the wood. Back in the field, I slid off him and wrapped my arms around his neck. How had it taken me so long to realise? It was like a veil dropping from my eyes. Albert was the unicorn in the story. He was the lost unicorn. He'd fallen through a tear in the invisible membrane and become separated from his mother.

I started to cry again, my tears mingling with the rain. "Don't worry, Albert. I'm going to help you. I promise. I'll find a way, whatever it takes." He whinnied softly, as I stroked his mane and kissed his nose. It was horrible leaving him. I glanced back as I climbed over the fence. He was watching me, his eyes deep and dark and full of fear.

I thought Mum would freak when she saw me. I was soaking wet and splattered with mud, but she barely seemed to notice. "Go and run yourself a hot bath," she said, "and then come down for dinner."

I took my sketch book into the bathroom while the bath was running and sketched the storm and the woods and the strange shadowy shapes, trying to make sense of what I'd seen. My heart ached at the thought of Albert all alone in the woods, searching for his mother. It was up to me to save him. It was up to me to make sure he found his way back home.

They told me about the operation at dinner. Mum explained that they didn't have a choice – the hospital had given them the date and there was nothing they could do. There would be a team of specialists from all over the country, so rearranging simply wasn't an option. They said the doctors were confident Boo would be fine and make a good recovery.

"Just think of it this way," said Dad. "In three weeks' time it will be over, and we can finally stop worrying."

The more they tried to reassure me, the more convinced I became that something terrible was going to happen. Last year on my birthday Granny Rae made Bakewell tart and Neve came round for a sleepover and we went bowling and out for pizza, and there was great excitement when Mum felt Boo move for the very first time.

This year, Boo could die.

Chapter Eighteen

Boo had two hospital appointments over the next couple of weeks in preparation for his operation. I persuaded Mum and Dad to take me to the first one. It was after school and I said I'd worry less if they let me come with them. It was Friday rush hour and the journey took ages. Boo wore himself out crying.

"Do that thing with your necklace," said Mum. "Remember last time? You practically hypnotised him."

My hand went up to my neck but my charm wasn't there. I'm not allowed to wear it to school. I leaned across to smooth Boo's hair out of his eyes and kiss his damp cheeks. He was hot and snotty, his little hands clenched into fists, pumping the air. He hated being in the car. And he especially hated this drive to the hospital.

In the waiting room I went straight over to the bookcase. I knew the book would be there without even looking, the same way I knew December 10th was jinxed. I pulled it out and curled up on one of the beanbags, blocking out the thought of Boo being pricked and poked and prodded as they got ready to cut open his chest and stop his heart.

The unicorn continued to train each day, returning to the woods to sleep. It was lonely in the field by himself. He missed his mother and the other unicorns, but he was determined to find the tear in the membrane and even more determined to be strong enough to get through when the opportunity finally presented itself.

One night, the unicorn was woken by a loud crash. He sprang to his feet. He knew that noise. It was the noise that had driven him away from his mother. It came again, and again, shaking him to the core. Rain fell from the sky, wind whipped through the trees.

He paced up and down, whinnying in fear, trembling all over. And then suddenly there was a flash. It illuminated the wood.

Illuminated the tear high above his head. Illuminated the shadowy world hidden behind the membrane. He reared up, and in that brief moment of light the unicorn saw his mother.

He charged at the membrane. He screamed for her, and he thought he heard her scream back. He screamed and screamed, over and over, desperate with grief and longing. And then it was dark again, and he was alone, and the brief glimpse of the world he'd lost was gone.

When the winds calmed and the rain stopped and the woods were quiet, the lost unicorn realised that galloping around the field was never going to be enough. Being tall and strong was never going to be enough. If he was ever going to find his way back to his mother, he would have to learn how to jump.

He realised something else as well. The next time he heard the loud crashing noise and the rain came down from the sky, he would have to be in the woods, close to where he first fell, ready for the flash of light that would show him the exact position of the tear in the invisible barrier.

In the car on the way home, Mum and Dad talked through the appointment. Boo had had lots of tests that all sounded the same: electrocardiogram, echocardiogram... I tuned out, thinking about the lost unicorn and the strange shadowy shapes I'd seen in the woods. I only had two chapters left to read. Two chapters for the unicorn to learn how to jump and then wait for another storm.

The weekend seemed to last forever. Mum wouldn't let Boo out of her sight, not even when he was sleeping. She would press temperature strips onto his forehead to make sure he wasn't hot and then do it again, ten minutes later, as if she couldn't trust the results. Dad kept offering to take over, but it was as if she couldn't trust him either.

Trish said Mum would give herself a breakdown if she carried on. She said it would be obvious if Boo had a temperature or if he was struggling to breathe. Mum didn't even bother arguing with her. I don't think she had the energy. I actually wanted her to get cross, or to tell Trish to shut up or to mind her own business.

Sheila came over on Sunday afternoon to see if Mum needed any help. Ruby was with her, wrapped in a baby carrier, kicking her chubby legs in the air. Mum wouldn't even to go to the door. "I wish she'd leave me alone," she muttered when she heard Dad chatting to her in the hall. "Just because we're neighbours doesn't mean we're going to be friends."

Belinda was late to school on Monday. She arrived in the middle of Maths. She looked terrible, like she hadn't slept all weekend or had her uniform washed or brushed her hair. When the bell rang for morning break, Miss Nightingale said she could stay in and help her sort through the new sports equipment that had arrived for the Winter Olympics if she wanted.

I asked Louise and Anisha about the Olympics on the way down to the playground.

"Oh, it's the best day," said Louise. "It's in the last week of term and we all wear Christmas jumpers and at the end we have hot chocolate with marshmallows. It's a tradition."

"So it's basically like sports day but in the winter?"

"Pretty much," she said. "You'll love it, Ariella, it's brilliant. Hey, do you remember that time in Year 4 when it started to snow?" She grabbed hold of Anisha's arm and they rushed ahead, remembering how the playground was as slippery as an ice rink and Lucas Jamieson went flying in the obstacle race.

Traditions were great if you'd been part of them from the beginning.

It was Topic all afternoon. We'd finished our

research and it was time to start work on the new business we were planning to open on the High Street. Belinda sat slumped to one side with her chin resting on her hand. I asked her if she had any ideas. We hadn't even chosen our business yet, but she just shrugged and made a face as if she couldn't be bothered.

Miss Nightingale came over to sit with us. "How about a nail bar?" she suggested. "I'm sure that would be popular. You like getting your nails done, don't you, Belinda?"

Belinda glanced down at her nails, chipped and chewed around the edges, and tucked them under the desk, shrugging again. "Or a pet shop?" said Miss Nightingale quickly. "For small animals, maybe, like hamsters and gerbils. You could call it Little Paws or Whiskers and Tails? Something like that?"

I waited for Belinda to make some joke about me being small – it was the perfect opportunity – but she opened her book and said, "Yeah, whatever, that's sounds okay. I'll do the writing."

Miss Nightingale beamed. "Great! Well, I'll leave you to make a start and come back to see how you're getting on in a bit." It was weird to think she knew about Boo being ill. I wanted to tell her about the operation and how it was on the same day as my birthday and how frightened I was, but not with Belinda sitting there.

Belinda opened her book and wrote PET SHOP FOR SMALL ANIMALS at the top of the page.

"What do you want me to do?" I still felt uncomfortable working with her. It was impossible to know what she was thinking, or when she might start picking on me again.

"Look up prices?" she said. "Things we could sell, like toys and food?"

We worked alongside each other without talking. It would've been such a fun project if Mr Major had paired me up with someone else. Neve would've loved it. She's got a hamster called Gus and I used to hold him whenever I went over there. He was so cute. He would burrow right into my chest.

He had this brilliant cage as well, with a whizzy exercise wheel and long, curvy tubes, like a mini theme park. It was exactly the sort of thing we could sell in our pet shop. I began to make a list of the different things we could stock: cages, food, toys, bedding and water bottles.

"I've never had a pet," said Belinda suddenly. "We're not allowed them where I live. It's rented and having a pet is against the regulations, or something."

I stared up at her, blinking through my glasses. Why was she telling me? Was she trying to be friendly? I seriously had no idea.

"I don't care anyway," she said, jutting her chin out. "I wouldn't want one. Not unless it was a horse, and that's never going to happen."

Chapter Nineteen

Every time I walked into a room, Mum and Dad stopped talking. The operation was only ten days away, but they hadn't said another word about the fact that it was on the same date as my birthday. And the more they didn't mention it, the more I worried about it, until it was impossible to think about anything else.

It was toasted cheese sandwiches again for dinner. "Can't we have some pasta or something?" said Trish. "I mean this is like, what, the fourth time we've had toasted sandwiches in the past two weeks?"

"Maybe you'd like to cook dinner one night?" snapped Dad. It was obvious he was about to explode but Trish didn't care.

"Make your mind up," she said, rolling her eyes. "Do you want me to revise more or do you want me to cook dinner for everyone?"

Mum was trying to get Boo to eat some specially fortified porridge, full of vitamins and minerals. He took a few mouthfuls and then pushed the spoon away. She tried again but he balled his hand into a fist and knocked the spoon flying.

"I'll go and get my necklace," I said. "It might distract him."

I swung the unicorn charm back and forth in front of his face, like in the car that time. He reached out for it, his eyes brightening but his lips stayed firmly shut.

"Come on, Boo," I pleaded. "Just one more spoon. It's yummy." I fastened the necklace around my neck and took the spoon from Mum. "Let me have a go. You never know. Maybe he'll take it from me."

I pretended the spoon was a train, and then an aeroplane, and then a horse galloping across a field. "Look, it's Ricky the Rocking Horse," I said in my best sing-song voice. "Here he comes, open wide." I made a galloping noise and bounced the spoon towards his mouth but it didn't work. Nothing worked. Mum took him up in the end. She said she'd try again later.

"One sandwich or two?" said Dad, carrying a plate over to the table. I shrugged, shaking my head. I wasn't hungry either. Whenever I thought about December

10th and Boo lying on the operating table, my tummy started to churn and burn, like when you put too much vinegar on your chips.

I had the worst dream that night. Boo was in the middle of his operation, but inside his chest there was a clock instead of a heart, and it was ticking really loudly, and when the hands reached twelve an alarm rang and the clock stopped ticking and none of the doctors could make it go again. They tapped it and shook it and wound it up, it but there was just this horrible, eerie silence.

I sat up, gasping. I thought it was the dream that had woken me until I realised I was wearing my unicorn charm and it was hot to the touch. I glanced at my clock. It was only ten but the house was quiet. I tiptoed over to the window, ducking under the curtains. Albert was in the field. Tall and white and majestic. I threw on a tracksuit and trainers and my warmest coat and crept downstairs. I didn't dare stop for carrots just in case Mum or Dad heard me in the kitchen.

I'd never been out so late by myself. The moon was big and round, lighting my way down the garden and through the blackberry bushes. As soon as I climbed over the fence, Albert came trotting over. It was the first time I'd seen him since the episode in the woods. He nuzzled my hands, searching for something to eat.

"Sorry, I haven't got anything. It was too risky." I was whispering even though no one could possibly hear me.

As my eyes adjusted to the dark, I realised someone else had been in the field. I looked around. There were red and white striped poles, some lying on the ground, others attached to stands, criss-crossed over each other to make different height jumps. And right at the furthest end, a towering wall.

It had to be Sheila. She said she owned the field that day up we were up at the High Street doing our survey. But why would she set up a jumping course when she didn't own a horse? "What do you think of this then?" I stroked Albert's nose. His eyes were wide open and staring. He'd never jumped before, as far as I knew.

We trotted around the edges of the field a few times. He was jittery, shying away from the fences, refusing to go anywhere near them.

"Come on," I said, nudging him with my knees. "Let's give it a go."

He went all the way round twice more before turning and trotting towards the single poles lying on the ground. They were only a few centimetres off the ground, but even so it was tricky to stay balanced when he hopped over them. "That's a boy!" I said, encouraging him to keep going. He was breathing hard, tossing his head from side to side.

He trotted back round and we had another go. It was the first time in ages that I felt like I needed a saddle and reins. I had to anticipate the moment he was going to jump and then lean forward, but not so far forward that I lost my balance.

We jumped the single poles again and again until I was confident enough to loosen my grip and sit up a bit straighter. Eventually we moved on to the two-pole jumps, and then the ones with three poles. I'd watched horse jumping on TV loads of times, but this seemed different. Once we were off the ground, it felt like we were flying.

Finally Albert cantered towards the wall. I clung tightly to his mane, my heart galloping as he picked up speed. "You can do it, Albert!" I cried, urging him on. We got closer and closer but at the last moment he jammed his hooves into the ground. It was lucky I was used to his emergency stops.

It took me a few moments to recover. I pulled myself back up to sitting, remembering how high the tear in the membrane was in the story, how high he would have to jump if he was ever going to get back to his own world. "You've got to have another go," I said firmly. "I know it's scary, but you've got to try."

He trotted back round and approached the wall for a second time. The same thing happened. Hooves jammed in the ground, me left hanging on round his neck. I urged him to have one more go. "Third time lucky, Albert. Don't give up now!" He made his way back round. "Come on, Albert! You can do it, I know you can. Come on."

He thundered towards the wall, mud spraying up around us. I tensed every muscle, leaned forward and braced myself for take-off, convinced this time he was going to do it, but at the very last moment he swerved off sharply to the right. It was so unexpected it was impossible to keep my balance. I shot off into the mud, rolling over and over.

Albert didn't slow down. He galloped round in a massive circle, bucking his back legs and rearing up. I curled into a ball, covering my face with my hands as he came charging back towards the wall, scared he might trample straight over me. I could hear him getting closer, clattering through the mud, closer and closer and then nothing.

I peeked through my fingers. He was standing over me, breathing hard, his eyes rolling back in his head so only the whites showed. "Don't worry," I said, reaching up to stroke his muzzle. "We'll keep practising. It's the first time we've ever tried." I pulled myself up and wrapped my arms around his neck. "I said I'd help you get home and I won't let you down. I promise."

Chapter Twenty

It was the third of December. Exactly a week until Boo's operation.

"Look what I've found," said Mum at breakfast. She held out a photo. It was me and Trish at the zoo. We're standing facing the monkey enclosure and Trish is holding my hand. "I was looking through all the old photos last night, photos of you two when you were little. I suddenly realised that we haven't made a single album of Boo as a baby…"

"Who took this?" I said. "Were you with us?"

"No, I was probably at work."

Mum used to work for a homeless charity before

Boo was born. She was in charge of all their fundraising events. She's still on her maternity leave at the moment. I think she was hoping to go back part-time when Boo was a year old, but I can't imagine that happening now.

"Look, I found this other one with it." Mum passed over the second photo. "You were with Granny Rae."

It was me and Granny Rae on the same day. She's looking straight at the camera but I'm gazing up at her.

"Doesn't she look fantastic?" said Dad, bringing a plate of croissants over to the table.

She did look fantastic. She was wearing a blue skirt with a blue and white striped shirt and a bright blue sun hat. Granny Rae loved her hats. She had a different one for every occasion. I stared at the photo. It was the first picture I'd seen of her since she'd died. I'd forgotten how stylish she was. How colourful she used to be before she got ill.

Trish came down a few moments later. She was holding her phone in one hand and my sketchbook in the other. It was open at the page where I'd drawn Albert and me jumping in the moonlight. "Here, you left this in the bathroom."

"It's private," I said, snatching it off her and stuffing it under the table.

"Well don't leaving it lying around then."

Dad opened his mouth to say something and then closed it again.

"Boo's never even been to the zoo," said Mum.

"You know, there's so much he hasn't done yet." Her face began to crumple. She'd probably been awake for most of the night.

"He's got loads of time to go to the zoo," said Dad quickly. "Years. He'll be out of hospital before you know it. What about your birthday, Ariella?" he hurried on, changing the subject. "You still haven't told us what you'd like to do."

"I don't want to do anything. Not on the day of Boo's operation."

"Not on the actual day, obviously." Dad glanced at Mum. "But we'll do something as soon as he comes home. We haven't forgotten."

"Maybe you could have a sleepover with one or two girls from school?" said Mum. "That should be easy enough to organise."

I felt my face flush. There were girls I'd like to invite, like Anisha and Louise, but I still hadn't been invited to any of their parties. And anyway, it would be ages after my actual birthday so it would just be weird.

"Or maybe you could have a unicorn party?" said Trish. "That would be fun!"

"Trish," warned Dad.

"I'm sorry," said Trish, "but seriously, believing in unicorns when you're almost eleven years old? It's pathetic!"

"Why were you even looking at my sketchbook? I told you it's private."

"Well if it's so private, why did you leave it wide open in the bathroom? Unicorns are *myth-i-cal* creatures, by the way." She smirked. "In case you didn't know, that means they're *not* real."

"Stop it, Trish," said Dad. "I mean it."

I stared at the photo of me and Trish at the zoo. I couldn't believe there was ever a time when she actually cared about me. Hot tears sprung up. "I don't care if Trish thinks I'm pathetic! She's so pathetic she doesn't believe in anything except her stupid phone! And how can you even ask me what I want to do for my birthday, anyway, when it's the day Boo's having his operation and he might die!"

"*Ariella!*"

I swung round to Mum. "Well it's true. I wish you'd both just admit it. He might actually die on my birthday and then every year for the rest of my life my birthday will be the day Boo died! Don't you get it? He might actually *die!*"

"*Ariella!*" Mum's face caved in. "How *could* you?"

I tore out of the kitchen and up to my room, away from Mum's tears. I'd only said what everyone else was thinking but didn't have the courage to say.

It was a few minutes until the bell. I was standing in the playground fiddling with the zip on my coat, close to a group of girls from my class. I wished there was someone I could talk to about Boo, a special friend waiting for me. None of them even knew I had a baby brother, let alone the fact that he was about to have a major operation.

"Surprise!" cried Miss Nightingale when we got up to the classroom. There were Christmas decorations everywhere. Paper chains criss-crossing the ceiling, sparkly silver tinsel lining the windows and a giant wreath hanging on the door. Everyone started talking at once, excited to see the classroom transformed. It was only three weeks until Christmas and I'd barely even noticed.

Last Christmas we were still in our old house. Granny Rae and Uncle Boris came over for lunch, like they always did, and I remember we had this big discussion about how the following year would be the baby's first Christmas. We worked out that he'd be ten months old and that he'd probably be crawling already. Mum said she'd be exhausted, chasing him all over the house, but she stroked her tummy as she said it, just as excited as the rest of us.

It's Creative Writing on Fridays. A whole hour to write whatever we want. Alex Fisher asked if he could write his Christmas list and Mr Major said that was fine as long as it had a well-structured beginning, middle and end and used lots of 'wow' words. Alex rolled his eyes, muttered 'boring' and pretended to yawn, and everyone laughed.

I spent the entire lesson sketching pictures of Albert in my book. I drew him in the woods, pressing against the invisible membrane. And then I did one of us jumping in the moonlight, and finally a picture of the woods during a storm, the hidden world of the unicorns illuminated by a flash of lightning.

I tore the pages out to stick into my sketchbook at home. I knew I'd be in trouble when Mr Major collected in the books and realised I hadn't done anything, and that I'd be in even more trouble when he saw the pages were missing. I picked at the bits of paper still stuck in the staples so it wouldn't look so obvious.

Miss Nightingale went around the room helping. I said I was fine whenever she came over to me, covering my book with my arm. Just before the bell she said that Belinda had written such a beautiful story she'd like her to share it with the rest of the class.

Belinda shook her head. "You read it if you want," she said, pulling a face. "I hate reading out loud."

Her story was about a girl who finds a wounded horse on a remote track and nurses it back to health, slowly gaining the horse's trust. My heart ached at the way she described the horse, half-starved, lying lame and frightened and in terrible pain. She sat with her head down the whole time Miss Nightingale was reading, biting the skin around her thumbnail.

"Maybe you'd like to help me decorate the tree?"

Miss Nightingale said to her when the bell rang and the others piled out of the classroom.

I asked if I could stay in as well. It was hard to know when I stopped being scared of Belinda. Maybe it was the moment I saw her at home cowering against the wall, or when she'd hidden behind me on the High Street. Or maybe it was just now, listening to her story.

Miss Nightingale talked about her kitten, Smudge, as we draped the tree in tinsel and hung up clay gingerbread men and red and white striped candy canes. She said she'd had to keep her decorations to a minimum at home because Smudge kept pulling them off or getting tangled up in the tinsel. She said the funniest was the way he reacted to the fairy lights, leaping in the air every time they flashed on and off.

Belinda didn't say anything the whole time. Close up she looked even worse than the other day. Her eyes didn't just have dark shadows underneath, they were red and swollen, and her fingers were raw around the edges where she'd bitten off the skin.

"I really loved your story," I said when Miss Nightingale went downstairs to bring the others up from the playground. "It was so sad." Belinda stared at me, not in a mean way but not in a friendly way either. "You must really love horses," I blundered on. "I love them too. I love all animals. We were supposed to be getting a dog when we moved but my mum's forgotten."

It was the most I'd ever said to her. Her eyes narrowed as if she was thinking, but she didn't say anything. The silence seemed to last forever. I picked up a piece of tinsel, twisting it around my hand, my face heating up.

"My mum's walked out," she said suddenly. "My sister's been looking after me for the past few weeks."

It was my turn to stare. "So you mean you don't know where she is?"

She shook her head. "No idea. And I can't even talk to her because she's not answering her phone. She's done it before. But never for this long."

She looked away as Miss Nightingale led the others into the classroom. I thought back to the Circle Time game, the one where we had to invent a spell. Belinda's spell was to find things that were lost. She said it was to help her find her keys or her favourite top. Maybe the real reason she invented it was so she could find her mum.

I didn't see Albert all weekend. I stood at my bedroom window, staring out into the empty field, wondering where he was. The jumps were still set up, some tall, some small, and right at the end of the course, the wall.

Chapter Twenty-One

The following week flew by in a blink. Every time Boo refused a feed or got too out of breath to finish, Dad would say, "Only five days to go." Then it was four, then three, two…and suddenly it was the day before, and Mum and Dad were taking him to stay overnight at the hospital for his final pre-op tests and checks.

I lay in bed winding the chain of my necklace round and round my finger until the skin turned white and then blue. Boo was leaving the house and he might never come back. I couldn't shake the feeling that when they stopped his heart to fix it, they'd never get it to start again, like the clock in my dream. I put my hand on my chest. If

I pressed very hard I could feel my own heart beating. It was going too fast. Ba-boom, ba-boom, ba-boom.

Dad called me down for breakfast. I got out of bed, my hand still pressed to my chest, the chain still cutting into my finger. The room spun around me and I nearly fell. I didn't want to say goodbye to Boo. I didn't want them to operate on him. My breath was coming too fast and then not fast enough. I was hot and cold and sweaty and scared.

"I can't breathe!" I cried, stumbling downstairs and bursting into the kitchen. "I can't breathe!"

I began to sob, clutching my heart, convinced I was going to die. I was gasping for air, but the more I gasped the less air went in. Dad led me over to a chair and sat me down. He crouched opposite me, holding my face in his hands. "You're not dying, Ariella, you're just panicking. I want you to keep your eyes on my face and copy my breathing."

He took an exaggerated, noisy breath in, and then a long breath out. I watched his mouth, felt his breath on my face. I tried to copy but it was difficult to take a deep enough breath.

"Keep going," he said. "Copy exactly what I do. Short breath in, long breath out. That's it, keep blowing out."

I took another breath and blew out. My heart slowed down a bit. It was easier to take the next breath in and the next. I sagged against him, tears streaming down my face. "It's okay," he said, stroking my hair. "It's all going to be okay."

"I don't want to say goodbye to Boo this morning. Let me come with you to the hospital. Please, Dad. He's used to me sitting next to him in the car. I'll read to him, sing songs, make sure he's okay, please, I'm begging you—"

"Okay, listen to me, Ariella. You need to calm down. You're getting worked up again. Let me go upstairs and talk to Mum. Will you be okay on your own for a moment?" He handed me a tissue and I nodded, wiping my face. I heard them talking at the top of the stairs. It was difficult to make out what Mum was saying. I unwound my chain and fastened it around my neck.

When Dad came back down he said they'd agreed I could come with them this morning, but I had to go to school tomorrow.

"It will be better for you to stay busy. It'll take your mind off things, and before you know it the operation will be over."

Boo was fine in the car. I read him *Ricky the Rocking Horse* and he squealed and giggled when I got to the *giddy up, giddy up* bit. I said it again and he squealed even louder and kicked his legs, his eyes fixed on my face, waiting for me to do it again.

"Not too much," warned Mum. "I don't want him to get overexcited."

I leaned over and buried my face in his. He giggled

and clutched hold of my hair. I breathed in his milky smell and rubbed my cheek against his and kissed his nose and his eyes and his soft cheeks, telling myself over and over that he was going to be okay.

The actual operation was in a completely different part of the hospital, but we had to go up to the heart clinic first for his final check-up and blood tests. I peeled away from Mum and Dad in the reception area and went over to the bookcase to find the unicorn book. I reached my hand through the row of books in front and pulled it out. It was like finding an old friend.

The lost unicorn was almost ready. He had taught himself to jump after discovering bales of hay in the field where he trained – some of them stacked high, one on top of the other. He was frightened at first. The bales towered over him, casting long, ominous shadows. But he soon realised he was an instinctive jumper, with good balance and a natural stride. The unicorn practised every day until he could jump all but the tallest tower. And at night he slept close to where he first fell.

It was winter and the weather was cold. The unicorn waited for another storm to pass over the woods. He pressed his body up against the invisible membrane and dreamed of his mother. 'It won't be long now,' he thought to himself. 'It won't be long before the loud crashing noise comes and the sky lights up.'

But there was something the lost unicorn didn't know. With each day that passed, the tear in the membrane was slowly mending. The fibres were knitting together, strand by delicate strand. It was only a matter of time before the hole closed up completely, trapping him on the wrong side of the barrier forever.

I gripped the book tighter, my heart beginning to beat too fast again. I had no idea the tear in the membrane was closing up. That it was a race against time. Albert still hadn't learned to jump properly – he couldn't clear the wall. If a storm came, he wouldn't be ready. He'd never make it.

I didn't want to read the last chapter. I didn't want to find out what happened to the lost unicorn when the next storm came. Not until I'd trained Albert to clear the wall. Not until I knew I'd done everything I could to help him find his way back home.

Mum brought Boo over for me to say goodbye. His face was red and blotchy. "I'm taking him up to the ward now," she said. "They're going to fit him with a feeding tube so they can give him a good boost of nutrition before the surgery."

I wanted to ask if it would hurt but I was scared of the answer. I followed her out to the lifts and we all stood there wishing we had more time. "I'll be back first thing tomorrow," Dad said to Mum, "but I'll speak to you later anyway. And let me know if you need anything."

They hugged and then Mum hugged me. She held me tight and told me not to worry. "I'll phone you in the morning to wish you a happy birthday," she said. "And it *will be* a happy birthday, okay?" I nodded, wishing I could believe her.

I bent down to Boo just as the lift doors opened to take us back to the car park. His face was crumpled as if he was about to start crying again.

"I'd better get him to the ward," said Mum. "He's exhausted, poor thing." I gave him one last kiss and pulled Dad into the lift. I didn't want to remember him crying.

It was impossible to fall asleep that night. Every time I closed my eyes, I imagined Boo lying in a hospital cot with the tube up his nose. And then I imagined him being wheeled down to the operating theatre, and then I imagined the doctors giving him an anaesthetic, then I imagined the moment they cut open his chest...

I gave up in the end and went downstairs to Dad. He was in the lounge with the news on. "I've spoken to Mum," he said, patting the space next to him on the sofa. "She said Boo was the most settled she'd seen him in ages after he'd had the nasal tube fitted. It was probably his first proper feed in weeks."

"Do you think it hurts?"

Dad shook his head. "I suppose it might be a bit uncomfortable but they're ever so narrow, the tubes, especially the ones they use for babies."

"What's actually going to happen tomorrow? Will you be at the hospital all day?"

"I'll drop you at school in the morning and then head off to the hospital. I've asked Sheila to be here for when you get home. I've given her a key and she'll stay until I get back."

"Sheila?"

"Yes, that's okay isn't it? I didn't want you and Trish waiting for news by yourselves. She said she doesn't mind how late it gets. She'll make you some dinner and keep you company."

I cuddled up to Dad just as the weather came on. It was going to be cold overnight, with a bitter, northerly wind. The weatherman pointed at the map and talked about freezing temperatures and morning frost. And then the map changed.

I sat up, leaning forward. There was an amber weather warning in place for tomorrow evening. A storm was coming in from the east, spreading across the entire country. It was due to reach us by the end of the day with strong winds and up to 10 cm of rain expected. A storm. That meant thunder and lightning. A chance for Albert to get back to his own world.

Except Albert wasn't ready.

And neither was I.

Chapter Twenty-Two

It took a few moments for me to remember it was my birthday when I woke up. It was early, just after six. The house felt empty without Mum and Boo. I got out of bed and went over to the window. Albert was already in the field. I banged on the glass and he raised his head. It was the best present.

I crept downstairs and took some carrots out of the fridge. The heating hadn't come on yet and it was freezing. I pulled my coat around me and slipped out the back door. It was just starting to get light. I stuffed my hands in my pockets and ran down the garden, my breath puffing out of my mouth like icy clouds, my feet crunching on the frozen grass.

Albert trotted over as I jumped down from the fence. I couldn't believe how tall and strong he looked, so different from the day I first saw him with his gangly legs and clumsy oversized hooves. "Hello," I said, holding my hand out flat so he could eat the carrots. "It's my birthday. I'm eleven years old today."

The air was crisp and still. It didn't feel as if a storm was on its way. Albert chomped and snorted his way through the carrots and then knelt down so I could climb on his back. He was calmer than the other night, less agitated. He trotted around the field once and then headed towards the first jump.

I was ready for him to stop dead or swerve off, but it was like riding a different unicorn. He must've practised while I was at school, or at the hospital, or sleeping. He timed every jump perfectly, as if he'd been jumping all his life. As if he'd been born to jump. He didn't falter once, not even as we approached the wall.

Adrenaline coursed through me as he thundered towards it. "Come on!" I cried. "Come on, Albert, you can do it!"

And suddenly we were in the air, sailing over as if he had wings, as if he could fly, landing on the other side without breaking his stride.

"Yes!" I cried, my heart bursting with pride and

happiness and relief. "You did it, Albert! You did it! You clever, clever boy!"

Afterwards we stood by the fence talking. I told him there was a storm coming later, that I'd heard it on the news. His ears pricked up and he looked away from me, across the field towards the woods. I stroked his mane. It was smooth and glossy. A part of me wanted to stay in the field with him forever, but I knew I had to let him go.

"You're ready now, Albert," I said, smiling through my tears. "You're ready to go home."

Dad was in the kitchen when I slipped back in. He looked creased and tired. "Ariella, you're freezing! What were you doing outside so early? You saw the weather forecast last night."

"I'm fine," I said. But my teeth were chattering and my hands were so cold they hurt.

"Come here," said Dad. He rubbed my hands between his, warming them up. "I'm going to make you the best birthday hot chocolate you've ever had, with the sweetest fluffiest marshmallows."

I'd begun to thaw out a bit by the time Trish came down.

"Happy birthday," she said handing me a gift bag. "I hope you like it."

I peered inside the bag. It was a scarf. Dark purple with white unicorns printed all over it. I pulled it out and wrapped it round my neck. It was beautiful. "I love it, thank you."

She shrugged. "It's no big deal."

I sipped my hot chocolate, peering at her over the rim of the mug. I had no idea if she was making fun of me, buying me something with unicorns on. It was impossible to tell with Trish.

Dad dropped me at school on the way to the hospital. There wasn't really time to say much. "Sheila will be waiting for you when you get back. She'll have all the latest news from the hospital, but I'll keep my phone on anyway and you can always call me later."

I gave him a quick kiss and then watched the car drive away, starting to feel cold all over again.

*

"Today is all about marketing," said Mr Major. "It's time to advertise your new business to the world. I'd like you to design a poster and write a press release, something that could appear in the local paper or online. Divide the tasks between you and then have a think about how you're going to present your business to the rest of the class."

We'd decided to call our pet shop Paws and Claws. Belinda got to work on the blurb while I made a start on the poster. It was a relief to be drawing. It was the only thing that helped take my mind off the operation. I tried out a few ideas in my rough book, sketching some of the pets we were planning to sell in our shop.

We hadn't got very far when Ms Gilmore came in and said she needed a word with Belinda in her office.

"Sorry to interrupt, Mr Major," she said. "It shouldn't take too long."

Belinda was gone for ages, almost the whole lesson. When she came back she slouched back to the table and turned to face the wall. Miss Nightingale asked her if she wanted to wash her face or get a drink, but she shrugged and said she was fine.

The poster was nearly finished. I'd drawn a picture of a pet shop window divided into six panes of glass with a different pet peeping out of each pane. There was a rabbit, guinea pig, hamster, mouse, chinchilla and tortoise.

"Oh that's so cute," said Anisha, coming over to have a look. "You're so good at drawing, Ariella."

My face started to heat up. I looked past her, out of the window. The sky was heavy, but there was no sign of wind or rain.

"I've got a hamster called Clive," Anisha went on. "He's really shy with other people, but not with me."

"Um…my best friend at my old school had a hamster," I said, squeaking like a hamster myself. No wonder I didn't have any friends at Baywood. I don't think anyone noticed I was there half the time.

"What's so great about hamsters anyway?" muttered Belinda. "They're basically small rats."

"Well, it's your shop," Anisha shot back. "You're the one selling them."

"It's not a *real* shop," said Belinda, sounding exactly like Trish. "If I could open a *real* shop I wouldn't waste it on something stupid like hamsters and rabbits."

Anisha made a face and went back to her table. Belinda carried on writing, but I noticed she was mostly rubbing out the same couple of words and rewriting them as if she was trying to make them perfect. I glanced at the clock. It was already two. The operation was scheduled for early afternoon. I forced myself to concentrate on the conversation with Belinda.

"What shop *would* you open then?" I said. "If it was a *real* shop."

Belinda was quiet for ages. Writing, rubbing out, writing, rubbing out. And then finally, as if we were having a completely different conversation, she said, "Someone on the estate reported us to social services. They know we've been left on our own. My sister's going to kill me when she finds out. She'll think it's all my fault."

Chapter Twenty-Three

It started raining on the way home. Sheila had come to meet me with Ruby and Maisy.

"We've made you a cake," said Sheila. "I haven't put candles on it or anything – I'm sure your mum will want to give you a cake with candles another time – but we couldn't let you go the whole day without a cake."

"Cake!" shouted Maisy, splashing in the puddles. She had ladybird wellies on and a little green umbrella that looked like a frog. "We maded you a cake!"

The kitchen smelled delicious. Warm and sweet and buttery. Sheila checked her phone and then checked it again just in case.

I watched her face. "Is there any news?"

She shook her head. "I haven't heard anything this afternoon. I only know that there was a slight delay, something to do with another operation, but it definitely wasn't cancelled. I presume he's still in theatre now."

I tried to eat some cake but my mouth was so dry it was impossible to swallow. Ruby was sitting in Boo's highchair. She was squashing raisins in her plump little hands and then dropping them on the floor.

"Maisy was very poorly a few years ago," said Sheila. "She had a really serious infection."

"Was it meningitis?"

Sheila nodded. "That's right, meningitis. At one point her temperature was so high she had a convulsion."

"Is that like a fit?"

"Yes. And it was very frightening. But I just had to trust the doctors, Ariella. I had to trust they would look after her. There was nothing else I could do."

I helped Sheila tidy up the kitchen and then she gave Maisy some tea. Maisy chatted non-stop about nursery and all her friends and how she'd helped her mum make my cake. It was still raining, heavier now, and the wind had picked up. "There's a storm coming later," I said to Sheila.

"I think it's already here. Have you seen how hard it's raining?"

"No I mean a proper storm with thunder and lightning. I heard it on the weather forecast last night."

Trish came home just before dinner. She was soaked. She said she'd just had a text from Dad. Boo was still in theatre and they were waiting for news. He said he'd call her as soon as they heard anything. Sheila put some pasta on to cook. Maisy and Ruby were in the lounge watching *The Little Mermaid*. By the time the food was ready, they were both fast asleep, Maisy on the couch, Ruby next to her, strapped into her baby seat.

We sat at the table, all staring at Trish's phone. The windows rattled in their frames. It was impossible to eat. Sheila asked Trish about college.

"It's been a nightmare concentrating," Trish said, "you know, with all this going on." She picked her phone up and put it down again. Her hands were shaking, her shoulders hunched up around her ears.

"I haven't told anyone at college about Boo. All my old friends know, obviously, but it's been easier to go to college and pretend none of it's happening."

It was like listening to a different person. She never gave the slightest impression she was even bothered about Boo being ill. Maybe she was just good at hiding it.

It was nine o'clock and we still hadn't heard anything from Dad. Sheila said we should do something to take our minds off waiting, watch TV or something. She carried Maisy upstairs to Mum and Dad's room. Ruby stayed downstairs, still sleeping in her baby chair. She looked even bigger than usual, way too big for the chair.

There was a cookery programme on. It was about making the perfect Christmas dinner. We sat in a row on the couch. The wind whipped around the house. It was so loud Trish had to turn the volume up so we could hear what they were saying.

We watched them do the turkey with this special apple stuffing, and roast potatoes and perfect little pigs in blankets, and then finally they got on to the pudding.

"I absolutely hate Christmas pudding," said Sheila. "I hate any cakes with raisins in."

"My Granny Rae used to make our Christmas pudding," I said. "She would throw one spoonful of the mixture onto the ceiling for luck."

Sheila laughed. "That sounds messy!"

"She always said if it stuck to the ceiling it meant there was going to be a good harvest. That's because she grew up on a farm in Russia. My Uncle Boris lived on the next farm. He still does. He usually comes over to spend Christmas with us, but not this year."

I wondered if I'd ever find out what Uncle Boris said to me after the funeral. I was certain it must be something to do with Granny Rae's unicorn charm being magic and Albert appearing in the field. It would be brilliant to tell him all about it – to tell him everything that had happened. I didn't realise when Granny Rae died that I'd lose Uncle Boris too.

Trish went upstairs before the pudding had finished

steaming. "I'll let you know if I hear anything from Dad," she said.

"Check on Maisy, would you?" said Sheila. "Although she's such a good sleeper, she could sleep through an actual tornado."

When the pudding was ready, they poured brandy over it and set it on fire. I watched the flames burning as the wind roared and the rain lashed against the windows and the old wooden frames rattled and, suddenly, over all the noise, like it was competing to be heard, there was an enormous clap of thunder. Ruby woke up, crying.

I jumped up. "I'm going to watch the storm from upstairs," I said.

"Are you scared?" said Sheila, lifting Ruby out of her chair.

"Not of the storm."

I raced up to my room. If there was thunder, there should've been lightning first. Lightning always comes before thunder. We learned that at my old school in Science. Light travels faster than sound. Maybe there was lightning, but I'd missed it. The curtains were drawn in the lounge and we'd all been staring at the TV.

I put my unicorn necklace on and stood at the window, straining to see through the rain and gloom. It was almost ten but I couldn't imagine sleeping. My charm felt warm against my skin. I wondered if Albert was in the woods, if the tear in the membrane was still open, if his mother was waiting for him on the other side.

The rain came down harder. The wind roared. I opened the window. I wanted to be closer to the storm, to feel it. I leaned out as far as I could, the rain soaking me in seconds, icy needles stabbing my scalp. The garden was wild, trees bent in half. Thunder rumbled on in the distance, and then finally, lightning. One mad, jagged, brilliant flash of light.

I gripped the window sill, blinking the rain out of my eyes. Albert was there. He was in the field. I could see him.

"Albert!" I screamed, but the wind swept my voice away into the night. "Albert! Albert! I'm up here! At the window! Albert!"

He was galloping round, racing at full speed, ears flat against his head. "Albert! Go to the woods, Albert! You've got to the go to the woods! The tear in the membrane is closing up! There's no time!"

I was shouting and crying and the clock was ticking and my heart was beating and the wind was moaning and the rain was lashing and the thunder rumbled, and finally, as the storm thrashed and crashed around me, he took off.

I held my breath, waiting, watching, straining to see into the distance, beyond the gate, down the lane, through the estate and into the woods. I imagined him going.

I imagined him pounding down the track, thundering back to his own world, back to his mother, waiting for him on the other side.

"Come on, Albert. Come on, you can do it, you can do it, you can do it."

I repeated it like a mantra, over and over and over, until the sky lit up again. A burst of electricity ripping through the inky night, illuminating the garden, the field, the world beyond. And seconds later, thunder. A deafening blast, a monster roaring deep within me.

"Ariella!" It was Sheila, running up the stairs, bursting into my room. "Ariella. Are you okay? I heard you shouting. What's wrong? Oh my God! What are you doing? Why have you got the window open? Come here! You're soaked through! Come here!"

And Trish bursting in behind her, waving her phone. "He's okay! He's through the operation! He's okay! Boo's going to be okay!"

Chapter Twenty-Four

I thought I'd never get to sleep. I was too keyed up. But as soon as I was warm and dry and tucked up in bed, my eyes began to close. It was still raining, but not as heavily as before. Just a steady beat drumming on the roof. The storm was over.

Sheila came up to check I was okay. She said she'd spoken to Dad. The operation was a big success. If Boo continued to do well tomorrow, he'd be transferred to a ward and we'd be able to go and visit him on Sunday.

"It won't be long now until they're home and you can put all this behind you, Ariella."

It was nearly lunchtime when I woke up. It was the

latest I'd ever slept. I lay in bed replaying everything that had happened: the storm, the lightning, Albert in the field. It was like a dream. I got out of bed and went over to the window. The garden was a mess. Like the morning after a wild party. The field was a mess too, the jumps lying flat and broken.

I went downstairs to make some breakfast. There was a note on the table from Dad. He'd gone to the shops to get a few things for Mum. I hadn't even heard him come home. I unwrapped the cake from yesterday and cut an enormous slice. I was starving. I took it back upstairs with a glass of milk and sat on my bed with my sketch book.

The last time I'd drawn anything was after Albert and I had jumped for the first time. The big full moon, the towering wall, Albert with his hooves stuck in the mud, too frightened to try. I leafed through from the beginning. It was more like a story than random sketches, starting on the day of Granny Rae's funeral when Uncle Boris gave me the unicorn charm.

I took a big bite of cake and sketched our second, more successful jumping session when Albert cleared the wall. *You did it!* I wrote in a big speech bubble. *You did it, you clever, clever boy!* And finally I sketched the storm. I gave the wind and the rain human characteristics, bringing them to life, wild and out of control, the wind rattling the window frames as it howled around the house, the rain lashing the trees.

The only part of the story I couldn't sketch was what happened to Albert after he left the field. I could imagine what happened, the way he pounded down the lane, through the estate and into the woods, the way he galloped towards the tear in the membrane, soaring through the air as if he had magnificent white wings, the way he greeted his mother on the other side.

I could imagine it, but I couldn't know for sure.

Dad told us everything when he got back from the shops. He said Boo was still in the intensive care unit and we wouldn't be able to visit until Monday after school. It was something to do with the tube in his throat and when it was due to come out. "He's awake though," said Dad, "and it's amazing, he's got more colour in his cheeks already."

The rest of the weekend was quiet. We played cards and watched TV and on Sunday night Dad took us out for pizza. It was the first time we'd done anything like that since we moved, we didn't even know where the local pizza place was.

I ordered a margherita from the children's menu but I was so hungry Dad let me get dough balls and a big ice cream sundae for pudding. I couldn't shove the pizza in fast enough. It was so hot and cheesy and delicious. The most delicious pizza I'd ever eaten in my life.

"God, slow down, Ariella. Boo's the one who hasn't been able to eat properly," said Trish.

"I haven't been able to eat properly either," I mumbled, my mouth stuffed full, realising it was true. "I've been so scared, my tummy's been hurting for weeks."

It was the last day of our projects on Monday. We had to gather all the information together and present it to the class. I assumed Belinda would take the lead when it was our turn, but she said she wasn't bothered. I held up the poster we'd made and explained how we were going to cater to anyone who already had, or who wanted to buy, a small pet.

I went through what we'd be selling in the shop and projected pictures of the cages and other toys and gadgets onto the whiteboard. As I played the PowerPoint presentation we'd made, talking through each slide as I went along, I realised that we'd ended up with a really good business.

When Mr Major invited the others to give feedback, Melanie Sykes said she thought it was a great name, and Louise said she loved the hamster cages and that she'd definitely buy one if she had a hamster. She then launched into a long story about why her mum wouldn't let her have a hamster because she said she'd only end up cleaning out the cage herself and she couldn't bear the smell, at which point Mr Major said no more feedback.

I sat down relieved it was over, but happy. Belinda had hardly said a word. She was hunched next to me, biting the skin around her thumb, dark smudgy shadows under her eyes. It must be so scary not knowing where your mum was or when she was coming home.

At the end of the day, Mr Major reminded us that it was the Winter Olympics on Friday.

"Make sure you've got your full PE kits, your Christmas jumpers and a bottle of water. I've looked at the forecast and at the moment they're saying it's going to be cold but sunny. We'll be in house teams like last year, so I'm expecting each and every one of you to step up and do your part. Remember our motto, 6M: *Together, everyone achieves more!*"

Miss Nightingale must've noticed the look on my face. "The Winter Olympics is great fun, Ariella. It's just like sports day, really. And you should see what we bought with the money from the cake sale – new batons for the relay and *proper* hurdles!"

Hurdles! Albert might be a natural-born jumper, but I'd never be able to clear a hurdle in a million years.

Chapter Twenty-Five

Dad was waiting for me outside school. We picked Trish up on the way and set off for the hospital. He said Boo had made good progress overnight and the tube had been removed from his throat.

"Does that mean he's completely fine now?"

Dad glanced at me in the mirror. "It's only been three days, Ariella, so try not to be too shocked. He's still got the nasal tube and various other tubes. And don't forget the scar on his chest, although it's got a big bandage on it at the moment."

It was the first time I'd been to the hospital without Boo in the car. I was nervous about seeing him but not nearly as scared as I was before the operation. We went up in the lift but along a different corridor towards the ward. I slipped my hand into Dad's and he squeezed it tight. Trish walked ahead of us. She didn't seem worried at all.

"Here they are!" cried Mum as we walked through the ward. She jumped up and rushed over, hugging Trish and then me, sort of shielding us from the bed. "Oh, I've missed you girls. You don't know how good it is to see you." She started to cry. "Happy tears!" she blubbed. "These are happy tears!" She turned round and led us over to Boo.

I started crying as soon as I saw him. I couldn't help it. He looked tiny lying on the enormous bed, and he had about a million wires and tubes coming out of his body like when Granny Rae was ill. Nothing could've prepared me. But then he saw us and he started smiling – the widest, happiest smile – and he kicked his skinny legs and pumped his fists.

We each went to one side of the bed. "Hello, Boo-Boo," I said, batting my tears away. I stroked his cheek and he clutched hold of my finger just like the day I first visited him after he was born.

"He feels strong," I said. "He *definitely* feels stronger." Trish took hold of his other hand and kissed it. She smiled at me across the bed.

"I know it looks scary, all the tubes and machines," said Mum, "but it's like a miracle. He's eating well and he's not nearly as tired as he was before. If he continues to make good progress, he'll be home before the end of the week."

"What, *this week?*" said Trish.

"Yes, and after that he won't need to come to the hospital again for six months. *Six months*, girls! Can you imagine? That's half a year. He'll be over one by then, he'll probably be walking and everything…"

The words bubbled out of her. It was brilliant to see her so happy. It had been so long. We were still sitting on either side of the bed talking and laughing when the nurse came to take Boo's temperature and check some other things.

"Why don't you take the girls down to the café?" Dad said to Mum. "I'll stay here with Boo. Go and get a coffee and get them a drink and something to eat. I meant to bring them a snack in the car but I ran out of time."

The café was on the same floor as the heart clinic. I asked Mum if I could check something in a book quickly and meet them in the café. She said she'd get me a sandwich and a juice and bring it to me.

It was weird being in the clinic by myself, without Mum and Dad and Boo. I kept my head down and went straight over to the bookcase, worried someone might ask me what I was doing there. I parted the books for the last time, slipping my hand through to the back.

A girl was sitting on one of the beanbags. She was about my age, maybe a year younger, with long, dark hair tied back in a ponytail. She didn't look ill except for the white plastic hospital band around her wrist. I sat on the beanbag next to her and she leaned over to see what I was reading.

"Oh, I love unicorns!" she said. "Where did you find that?"

"I've only got one chapter to go," I said, "and then I'll give it to you, if you like."

The unicorn woke just before midnight. He wasn't sure if it was the driving rain, the flash of light or the booming clap of thunder that had disturbed his sleep. He began to tremble, frightened at what lay ahead. He'd jumped the tallest tower of haystacks, but what if the tear in the membrane was higher? What if it was still out of reach?

He stumbled through the trees and out of the woods. He needed more practice – one final jump to give him courage. He was scared of the storm. Scared he'd never see his mother again. Scared he'd be trapped on the wrong side of the invisible barrier forever.

Pounding down the track blinded by the rain, the storm raged on. There was a flash of lightning and then another. He reached the field and saw the haystacks strewn across the grass, the tower destroyed. He galloped around, eyes wild, ears flat against his head. The sky lit up again and he knew he had to get back.

The wind drove him down the lane. It propelled him through the estate and into the woods. There was another flash. He could see the shadowy shapes, the world of the unicorns on the other side of the barrier, but where was the tear? He swung his head in terror, crying out for his mother.

The rain lashed and the thunder crashed, shaking the ground beneath him, but above the deafening cacophony of the storm, he heard her answer. And when the next flare of light lit up the sky, he knew exactly where to jump.

No one knows how the lost unicorn made it through to the other side. It remains a mystery to this day. One moment he was there, soaring through the sky like a magnificent white bird, and a moment later, like a magician performing his greatest trick, he had gone.

"Here you go, Ariella." It was Mum. "I've got you tuna and sweetcorn. I hope that's okay?"

I glanced up, desperate to read the last few pages. "Hang on a minute. I've just got to finish this."

Mum hovered next to me. "I've left Trish in the café. What's so important?"

I held the book up to show her. "I've been reading it every time Boo's had an appointment and I'm on the last bit."

Mum took the book out of my hand. "I don't believe it."

"What?"

"It's Granny Rae's book. You're reading Granny Rae's unicorn book."

I stared at her. "What do you mean Granny Rae's book? I found it here, at the back of the bookcase."

Mum shook her head. "After Granny Rae died, I had to clear out her flat. I put it off for weeks. It was really painful. I bagged up most of her things for the charity shop. I didn't really see what else I could do with them. There was a box of really old books, adult books, mainly, that she must've read about a hundred years ago, but among them was this one children's book."

"It was actually *in* Granny Rae's flat?"

Mum nodded. "I was coming to the hospital later that day with Boo for one of his check-ups, so I brought it with me and asked them if they'd like it for their book corner."

"I knew I'd heard it before! Granny Rae used to tell me this story at bedtime when I was little, it's about a lost unicorn, but I don't remember her ever reading it to me from a book. She must've known it off-by-heart. But it's the weirdest thing, it doesn't say who wrote it or anything..."

"Perhaps Granny Rae wrote it herself when you were a baby, or maybe when Trish was, or even way back when I was a little girl." Mum looked inside the front cover and then flicked through the pages. "It wouldn't surprise me, to be honest. She always had such a fantastic imagination. She used to tell me the most amazing stories when I was growing up."

She handed it back to me.

"Maybe you should bring it home, Ariella. I wasn't thinking straight when I brought it here. I was so tired and emotional."

I started to nod. I already felt like it was mine anyway. But then I looked across at the girl with the long dark hair and the hospital tag around her wrist and shook my head.

"I've got a feeling Granny Rae would be happy for it to stay here, for other children to read. She always said stories were for sharing. And anyway, I've only got a couple of pages left..."

Mum said she'd meet me back in Boo's room and went off to find Trish. I couldn't believe I was almost at the end of the story. I wanted to savour every last word, especially now I knew *The Lost Unicorn* belonged to Granny Rae, and that there was even a chance she'd written it herself.

By the time the lost unicorn was reunited with his mother, the storm had passed over the wood and the last remaining fibres of the tear had knitted themselves back together.

"Albert!" she cried when she saw him. "My little Albert! My precious foal! I thought I'd lost you forever!"

The unicorn told his mother about his time on the other side of the membrane. He told her how much he'd missed her and how difficult it had been to find his way back. He knew he would never forgot the time he'd fallen through the tear – the long days and lonely nights, the fear and hunger.

The little unicorn was tall now, and strong – one of the strongest unicorns in the herd. The other unicorns looked up to him. No other unicorn had ever gone through the barrier and survived. But when a storm next passed over the woods, he made sure to stay close to his mother. And when the thunder rumbled and the wind moaned and

the sky lit up, he caught a fleeting, shadowy
glimpse of the world he'd left behind on the
other side.

I closed the book, hugging it to my chest. Albert had
made it back. After everything he'd been through, he
was back home with his mother where he belonged.
The girl with the long dark hair was watching me,
waiting for me to finish.

"I hope you enjoy it," I said, holding it out.

"Is it sad?"

I nodded. "It's really sad. But don't worry, it's got
a happy ending."

Chapter Twenty-Six

Mr Major was right about the weather. By lunchtime on Friday it was sunny but icy-cold. Easily the coldest day of the year so far. I thought about pretending I'd forgotten my PE kit to get out of the Winter Olympics, but there was always the chance I might have to wear something horribly embarrassing from lost property.

We got changed straight after lunch. I didn't have an actual Christmas jumper but Mum had dug out a sparkly white cardigan that used to belong to Trish. In the end it was Belinda who didn't have her kit. She said it was in the wash, shrugging as if it was no big deal. Miss Nightingale took her down to the office and they came back a few moments later with an oversized pair of shorts and an old white t-shirt.

When we got onto the field, some special helpers handed out coloured bands to show what house we were in. I took my blue band and went to sit with the rest of my team, seriously doubting whether I'd score any points for them at all. All the parents had been invited to watch. Mum said she'd come if she could, but there was no sign of her yet.

Boo had been home since Wednesday. It was amazing how quickly he'd recovered from the operation. Mum said it was because his heart was finally working properly so he had far more energy than before. It would still be a few weeks before he was allowed out or anything like that, but he'd already put on weight. He seemed to be hungry all the time.

I trailed over to the first event, javelin. We had to throw this foam arrow-thing across one section of the field, and the furthest distance won. My throw was pathetic. The javelin more or less landed at my feet. The sack race wasn't much better. The sack was so big it was impossible to move forwards without tripping over. "Come on, Ariella!" shouted the rest of the blue team, urging me on. But it took me twice as long as anyone else to get to the finish line.

I kicked off the scratchy sack, looking round for Belinda, half-expecting her to be standing behind me laughing. She hadn't actually teased me about my height for weeks but today was the perfect opportunity, especially since she was in Reds and according to Lucas Jamieson they always won.

"That looked tough, Ariella." It was Miss Nightingale. "Never mind, it's the hurdles next. The *new* hurdles. Have you seen them? They're brilliant."

I stared up at her. If I couldn't do the sack race, how did she expect me to do the hurdles? *I'm rubbish at jumping,* I felt like saying, *apart from when I'm riding Albert.* If only Albert were here right now. A Winter Olympics for unicorns. Bareback riding around the field, cross country through the woods. We'd smash every event.

By the time I'd finished falling over the 'brand new' hurdles, I saw Mum had arrived. She was standing with some of the other mums. She gave me a thumbs up and waved me over.

"Dad's looking after Boo," she said. "I was just showing Louise's mum some photos on my phone, explaining why I haven't been up at school much."

"Your brother is seriously cute," said Louise's mum. "I'm so pleased he's on the mend."

Just then Louise and Anisha came racing over to us.

"Oh, is that your baby brother, Ariella?" cried Louise, taking the phone from her mum. "He's soooo cute!"

"Hello, girls," said Mum. "You look like you're having fun. How's it going?"

"It's freezing!" said Louise. "Can you believe we have to wear shorts in this weather? But at least we get hot chocolate at the end."

"We didn't know you had a baby brother, Ariella," said Anisha, taking the phone from Louise to look.

"He's been really poorly," said Mum. "He had to have a big operation, but he's doing much better now."

Anisha scrolled through the pictures and then handed the phone back to Mum. "You're so lucky, Ariella. I wish I had a baby brother or sister!"

I looked at her, surprised. I certainly hadn't felt lucky since Boo was born. Moving house, changing schools, Mum and Dad exhausted and worried all the time.

Louise grabbed Anisha's arm before I could say anything. "Come on, we'd better go or we'll miss the next event."

"Good luck," called Mum as they ran off. She gave me a quick hug. "They seem nice."

That's when I noticed Belinda. She was standing just across the track, staring at us. I stared back, knowing she wouldn't do anything, not with Mum there. She already had two stickers on her t-shirt to show she'd won her first two events. She'd probably been looking forward to the Winter Olympics as much as I'd been dreading it.

I took my place at the start of the obstacle race. There were four of us competing against each other, one from each house. Alex and Freddy were on my left and Melanie was on my right. The first obstacle was a narrow beam. You had to run from one end to the other without falling off and then drop down to crawl under the army-style netting. Beyond that, were some bucket stilts to finish the race, two upside-down buckets with handles made out of rope.

"On your marks!" Mr Major lifted the whistle to his mouth. "Get set!" Freddy put his foot on the bench. "Go!"

I jumped straight onto the bench, sticking my arms out to keep me steady. It didn't take long to get to the end. It was easy compared with balancing bareback on Albert. It was only when I looked round that I realised the other three had all fallen off and were back near the beginning.

"Come on, Ariella!" shouted Mum, along with some other children wearing blue bands.

I jumped off the beam and crawled under the net, not quite believing I was actually in the lead. All the time I'd spent in the field with Albert was paying off. Apart from improving my balance, I was way stronger than I used to be. I clawed my way along the ground as fast as I could, and as I pulled myself out the other side I looked back and saw that Alex and Freddy had only just made it off the beam and Melanie had given up entirely.

Some of the blue-band girls were chanting, "A-ri-e-lla! A-ri-e-lla!" and "Blues, Blues, never lose!"

I stepped up onto the brightly coloured bucket stilts

and grabbed the handles. It was the last part of the race. Suddenly I was taller than I'd ever been and it felt amazing. I took off down the field towards the finish line as if I were Albert galloping back to the woods on the night of the storm.

It was tricky to run on the buckets, especially as the grass was full of tufty clumps and muddy patches. I nearly fell off a couple of times but just about managed to steady myself without slowing down. I was determined to keep going. It was the only chance I had of winning anything the whole afternoon.

Mum had run down to end of the course. Miss Nightingale was already there. "Come on, Ariella!" they cheered. "Come on!"

Winning the obstacle race at school wasn't like winning a gold medal at the real Olympics but that's exactly how it felt as I crossed the finish line. I jumped off the stilts, punching the air, as one of the helpers swooped over to give me a winner's sticker. My first one ever.

"Way to go, Ariella!" cried Miss Nightingale. "I don't think anyone's completed the obstacle race without falling over at least once! You were awesome!"

I ran over to Mum in a daze.

"What just happened?" said Mum, laughing. "When did you get so good at balancing? I wouldn't be able to take two steps on those stilts without falling over, and you practically flew down the beam. It must be all that playing outside. I bet you've been training in secret!"

"Don't be silly," I said, but my cheeks ached I was grinning so hard.

At the end of the afternoon, the Parents' Association handed round hot chocolate with marshmallows. I sat with Mum, warming my hands on my cup, checking every now and then that my sticker was still on my t-shirt. Belinda was sitting on the other side of the field with Miss Nightingale. And then I realised. She'd had nobody there to see her win.

Chapter Twenty-Seven

Suddenly there was no stopping Boo. He became an eating machine. I'd got so used to him sucking on the same bottle of milk, falling asleep halfway through, turning his head away when Mum tried to feed him anything solid. Now he was hungry all the time. It was amazing how different he looked. More like a little boy than a baby.

It was the last three days of school before the Christmas holidays. We didn't do any proper work. We made Christmas cards and watched the infant nativity and sang carols in assembly. Melanie's dad dressed up as Santa and came round to every class with presents. I got a Christmassy writing set – pencil, pen, ruler and rubber – and a chocolate bauble.

It was our class party on Monday afternoon. Everyone brought in food and then after we'd eaten we did games in the hall. Belinda didn't even come down. She stayed in the classroom and helped Miss Nightingale tidy up. I hadn't spoken to her since before the Winter Olympics. I didn't really know what to say.

When I got home from school, I noticed Mum's recipe book was out and there were some ingredients on the side. A box of eggs, a packet of ground almonds and a jar of raspberry jam. I went upstairs to find out what was going on.

Mum was in her room with the curtains drawn but she was awake, propped up in bed drinking a cup of tea. "I was just grabbing five minutes peace while Boo's napping. I've got some good news. I spoke to Sally this morning and she's going to bring Neve down next Sunday to spend the day."

"Do you mean it?"

Mum nodded. "Oh, and I thought we could do some baking together, have a go at Granny Rae's Bakewell tart. We haven't done anything like that for ages."

The moment Mum said Bakewell tart it was like Granny Rae was in the room with us, making everything better again. "Why don't you stay in bed and have a rest?" I said. "I'll make it. I made it so many times with Granny

Rae, I'm sure I'll remember what to do."

Mum smiled. I wondered if she could feel it too. "Well, if you're sure, sweetheart. I think I'm still catching up with all the sleep I lost last weekend. And you never know, maybe your sister will give you a hand."

"Trish? Help me bake?"

"I know she's a moody mare at the moment, but trust me, Ariella, the real Trish is still in there somewhere!"

I'd just started measuring out the flour when Trish arrived home from college. She came straight into the kitchen to get a drink, eyeing the ingredients on the worktop.

"I'm making Granny Rae's Bakewell tart, if you want to help?" I said. "The one with raspberry jam."

After a moment's pause that felt more like an hour, she dropped her bag. "Alright. I don't mind helping. But only if I can have some at the end."

Trish seemed to know a lot more about making Bakewell tarts than I realised. She knew which tin to use, and how to blind bake the pastry with beans to stop it puffing up. She even knew how to line the tin with greaseproof paper, cutting the edges so they fitted just right.

"I used to make this with Granny Rae before you were even born," she said, rolling her eyes. "There was life *before* Ariella, you know."

I stared up at her, surprised. It was always me and

Granny Rae. Trish was too busy doing other stuff. Netball or swimming or hanging out with her friends.

"I asked Granny Rae once why she loved making Bakewell tart so much," Trish went on.

"And she said that even though she would always feel Russian in her heart, Bakewell tart was the one recipe that made her feel she belonged in England too."

Mixing the sugar, almonds and eggs into the warm melted butter, an idea started to grow. If making Bakewell tart helped Granny Rae feel she belonged in England, maybe I could take one into school to share with everyone as a sort of belated birthday celebration. Maybe sharing the Bakewell tart would finally help me feel as if I belonged at Baywood.

We doubled the mixture and Trish began to talk about college and how difficult it had been at first, making new friends, starting over from scratch. Her phone pinged every few seconds with messages and updates, but she ignored them. She wanted to know how Baywood compared to our old school, Stanley Road Primary.

Trish was already in Year 6 when I joined Stanley Road in Reception. I remember being super-proud she was my big sister, especially when she was in a play or speaking in an assembly. And I loved it when our classes were buddied up for reading sessions and other activities.

The kitchen began to smell sweet and buttery. We made the tart for school in a rectangular-shaped tin so

I could cut it into thirty equal pieces, and we made the family one in a regular round tin. By the time Mum came down, both the tarts were in the oven.

"That smell," said Mum, closing her eyes. "It's almost as if Granny Rae is right here with us."

I knew exactly what she meant but it didn't make me sad. Following Granny's recipe had brought me and Trish together, even if it only lasted until Mum mentioned the washing-up.

"Sorry, but I've got a massively important presentation to finish for tomorrow," Trish said, heading straight for the door and disappearing in a cloud of flour.

"Typical," said Mum. "She'll soon come rushing down when she wants a slice."

Mum and I cleared up together. She talked about Granny Rae and the first time *they* made a Bakewell tart together. I bet Granny Rae would love to know we were still following her recipe, that it was still working its magic, even though she wasn't here to bake it with us.

When the tarts were ready, Mum took them out of the oven and we left them to cool on a wire rack. They looked amazing and smelled even better. Trish came down to see how they'd turned out. She picked off a bit of pastry from the edge and then took a photo and posted it online with the caption, *Me and my little sis made Granny Rae's Bakewell tart.*

Chapter Twenty-Eight

No one at school knew I'd already had my birthday. It felt weird announcing it suddenly out of the blue. I took the slices of Bakewell tart straight inside to Miss Nightingale and asked her if she could mention it at the end of the day without making a big fuss.

"Is this what you were going to make for the cake sale?" she said, peeping inside one of the tins. "It looks delicious!"

I nodded, pleased she'd remembered. "I used to make it with my Granny Rae."

"Isn't that lovely, when a recipe gets passed down from one generation to the next."

I smiled to myself. The recipe wasn't the only thing Granny Rae had passed down.

"Hey, I bet your Granny Rae would make a big fuss of you if she were still alive. Are you sure you don't want everyone to sing you a belated happy birthday?"

"I really, really don't."

"Well, let me make a fuss at least."

She started singing in a silly voice, like an opera singer. "*Happy birthday to you! Happy birthday to you! Happy birthday, dear Arieeeeella…*"

I couldn't help giggling. She sounded so funny.

"I've got something for you, actually," she said when she'd finished. "I've just printed it out. You can take it home as a belated present."

It was a picture of me winning the obstacle race. I'm standing on the plastic buckets, hands gripping the strings, blue band across my chest, crossing the finishing line with the biggest grin on my face.

We spent most of the morning clearing out our desks and getting the classroom ready for next term. Our new Science topic was 'habitats'. It sounded brilliant. We were going to do pond-dipping, sketching and classifying plants, and we'd even be designing and creating our own wildlife garden.

But the most exciting part was that we were going to go to the woods to learn how to build a shelter. Even Mr Major seemed excited. He said that since we were lucky enough to have a wood on our doorstep, it would be a waste not to use it as a base for our studies.

My old school was in the middle of the city. It hardly had a proper playground, let alone a wood nearby. And we never did any lessons outdoors. I already knew the woods so well, I'd spent so much time in there with Albert. For the first time since we moved, I might actually know as much as the others.

Just before the bell rang at the end of the day, Miss Nightingale stopped everyone and told them I'd brought in a Bakewell tart to celebrate my birthday. She called me up to the front and said I should choose someone to help me hand it out. A bunch of people volunteered, including Louise and Anisha.

I looked over at Belinda. She was staring out of the window as if she hadn't even heard. She suddenly seemed more alone than me. Maybe she'd been more alone all along but was better at hiding it from the others than I was. "I'd like Belinda to help me," I said. "If she wants."

If Miss Nightingale was surprised, she didn't show it. "Lovely," she said. "Just don't forget to save a piece for me!"

Belinda didn't seem surprised either. She was probably too worried about her mum to care one way or the other. We stood side by side at the door, each holding a tin. Eventually everyone had taken a piece of tart, wished me happy birthday (even though it wasn't actually my birthday) and skipped off out of the classroom.

Miss Nightingale was dismissing children in the playground by the time we got down there. I handed her the last piece of tart and she gave me a quick hug and said I was a lovely girl and she was so pleased I'd joined Baywood Primary. When I looked up, I saw Belinda was waiting for me by the gate as if we'd been walking home together for years.

"What are you doing for your birthday?" she said on the way out. "Louise had a riding party, but that was ages ago."

I hesitated. "My birthday was over a week ago. I couldn't actually do anything on the day because my baby brother was in hospital having an operation."

We carried on in silence. When we got to the fork in the lane, she stopped, scuffing the ground with her foot.

"They're not going to let my sister look after me. She's only sixteen and it's against the law or something. She's so stressed out she shouts at me all the time anyway."

"What will happen? Will you have to move away?"

"I'm not sure. My nan might be able to come and look after us but she's been poorly."

I took a quick breath. "Why don't you come back to my house for the afternoon? It's just down the lane and across the field. You can stay for tea, if you like. My mum won't mind."

Sheila was over visiting Mum. They were having coffee in the lounge. Ruby and Boo were on the floor playing with a big pile of coloured bricks, banging and squealing, while Maisy lay on her tummy colouring in.

Mum asked me how the day had gone and if I'd remembered to bring the tins back. "We've just had a slice of the tart ourselves. It was delicious. And look at these two, getting on so well. Ruby might be younger, but she's not taking any nonsense from Boo!"

Belinda stood at the edge of the room, looking uncomfortable.

"Have you been down to the field recently, Ariella?" Sheila said suddenly.

I shook my head, blushing. "Not since the night of the storm."

"Listen, there's not much light left, but why don't the two of you go down there now?" I stared at her, confused. "Oh and you might want to take a couple of carrots, if your mum's got any."

"Carrots?" I said.

"There are loads of carrots," said Mum. "I've been buying double the amount I usually do since Ariella decided they're her favourite food."

I led Belinda out into the garden, both of us clutching a carrot in each hand.

"What was your mum's friend talking about?" she said as we ran down the lawn. "What are the carrots for?"

But I couldn't answer. My mouth was too dry, my heart thudding.

"This way," I muttered, when we got to the bottom. I helped her through the tangle of blackberry bushes, careful to dodge the stinging nettles. We stuffed the carrots in our pockets and climbed up the fence, leaning over the top. The field looked exactly the same as before the storm. Sheila had fixed the jumps, including the wall. Was that what she wanted me to see?

"Ariella, look!" breathed Belinda. "Over there!" She pointed across the field.

A white horse was trotting towards us. The most beautiful white horse I'd ever seen. I watched him approach, head held high, proud and sure of himself. He was taller than Albert, bigger and stronger-looking, with a long, flowing mane.

"I don't believe it," said Belinda. "You didn't tell me there was a horse in the field."

We jumped down as he got closer, standing with our backs pressed against the fence. Belinda pulled a carrot out of her pocket.

"Hold your hand out flat like this," I said, showing her.

"I know what to do," she said. "I love horses, remember?"

The horse came right up to us, tossing his head and blowing out of his nose. He sniffed out the carrots in no time, and his velvet lips brushed over my hand first and then Belinda's as he munched and crunched.

"It tickles," said Belinda, giggling. I realised it was the first time I'd ever heard her giggle. I'd heard her laugh in a mean way, but I'd never heard her giggle. It sounded strange. Like she was a different person.

"I wonder what his name is?" she said. "I'd call him Casper. Do you think your neighbour will let us come down here and see him again?"

I stroked the horse's nose, staring into his soft, chocolate-brown eyes and smiling as his breath warmed my hands. "I'm sure she will. Maybe she'll even let us ride him one day."

Mum said she'd walk Belinda home after tea. She pushed Boo in the pram while Belinda and I ran ahead. We talked about the horse the whole way, planning when we could next go to see him. We talked and talked and it was strange how normal it felt, as if we'd been friends for a very long time.

"Did you have fun?" said Mum on the way back.

"It was brilliant, especially going down to the field."

"Belinda seems really nice."

"She is," I said, realising Mum had no idea how mean Belinda used to be. "I just hope her nan can come and look after her so she doesn't have to move."

"I can't even imagine how awful it must be for them," said Mum. "Those poor girls.

"Sheila seems nice too," I said, gently hitting Mum on the arm. "Now you've actually decided to be friends with her."

"I know, I know. I was horrible. I was jealous, to be honest, Ariella. Jealous that she had such a healthy little girl. I'm lucky she was understanding enough to give me another chance."

"So we've both got a new friend."

We talked about Christmas the rest of the way back. Mum said we could get a tree on Saturday and do some shopping.

"Oh, and that reminds me," she said, pulling something out of her bag. "This arrived for you earlier today."

It was a postcard from Uncle Boris. I stopped for a moment, running my eyes over it. "He's coming for Christmas!" I said. "Next week, Mum! He's coming *next week!*"

Mum nodded. "I know. And he's going to stay with us as well. I actually spoke to him a few days ago, after the operation. I didn't tell you because he told me he'd sent you a postcard and I didn't want to spoil the surprise."

I started to laugh. "I don't believe it!" At the bottom of the card were the mysterious Russian words he'd said to me at the funeral, *uvidimsya na rozhdestvo.* And next to them, clear as anything, the English translation. *See you at Christmas.*

All he'd done earlier that year was lean in close to me at the bottom of the stairs and say 'See you at Christmas' – and all this time I'd been thinking there was some big mystery. Once I started laughing, I couldn't stop. I laughed and laughed and laughed, and Mum caught my laughter and started laughing too until we were clutching hold of each other, gasping for breath.

I was back in my room, sketching my afternoon with Belinda. I'd just got up to the bit where we saw the white horse trotting across the field towards us when Dad came in. He asked if I'd mind reading Boo a story to help him settle. He'd cooked something special for Mum (not tinned tomato soup *or* toasted cheese sandwiches) and they were looking forward to a peaceful evening together.

Boo began jumping up and down in his cot as soon as he saw me. He didn't look very sleepy. I lifted him out and sat him on my lap on Mum and Dad's bed, cuddling him close. He smelled of baby bubble bath and warm milk.

"I'm going to tell you a story," I said. "A magical story all about a unicorn called Albert…"

We asked Anne-Marie some questions about writing *Unicorn Girl*...

Where did the idea to write the story come from?

At the school where I work as a drama teacher, I think it's fair to say some of the girls are unicorn-crazy. I really wanted to write a story for them, but I needed an idea. And then one day, one of the girls told me that her gran had died and left her a necklace....

How do you think Albert helps Ariella?

He helps her to feel less lonely, but he also helps her to feel more confident. Starting a new school has been so difficult for Ariella, especially with her baby brother so poorly. Learning how to ride Albert, and then helping him find his way back to his own world, gives her a massive boost.

When do you think Ariella stops being scared of Belinda?

From the moment Ariella realises that Belinda was the girl she saw cowering against the wall, she begins to see Belinda in a new light. She comes to understand that Belinda is not as confident as she makes out, and that in her own way she's just as lonely as Ariella is herself.

Trish is really mean to Ariella. Do you have a big sister?

I do have a big sister, but she isn't mean at all. She's my best friend!

Do you believe in unicorns?

Of course! Don't you?

Find out more about Anne-Marie Conway and her books at:

https://amzn.to/2NZ1LLM
www.anne-marieconway.tumblr.com

'Butterfly Summer'

In her summer of secrets, all Becky knows is that everything can change in the beat of a butterfly's wing…

Winner of the Oxfordshire Book Award 2012

When Becky finds an old photo in a box under her mum's bed, everything she thought she knew comes crashing down. The only place she finds comfort is at the Butterfly Garden with her new friend, Rosa May. But with her wild ways, and unpredictable temper, is Rosa May hiding something as well? In the heat of the sun-drenched summer, it seems that Becky is the only one in the dark…

'Forbidden Friends'

The unforgettable story of a new friendship, a terrible tragedy and a long-buried lie.

Winner of the Southwark Book Award 2019

When Lizzie and Bee meet on holiday, it feels as if they were always meant to be friends. Escaping their parents and exploring, everything seems perfect in the hot summer sun. But as the two girls grow closer, strange questions rise to the surface…Is Lizzie really an only child? Why has Bee's dad disappeared? And why, as the holiday comes to an end, are the two girls forbidden from seeing each other again?